An

Even in the darkness of the room, he could see that they were shimmering with desire. The blinds were open, allowing moonlight to spill into the bedroom. The vision of Salina on the bed, ready to make love with him, made his breath catch.

He wanted this. But he had to make sure that she wanted it, too. "Are you sure?"

In response to his question, Salina sat up and pulled the robe off of her body. All she wore now was an oversize T-shirt. Nothing had looked as sexy on a woman. No lace bra, no thong underwear—absolutely nothing.

"I'm sure."

Books by Kayla Perrin

Kimani Romance

Island Fantasy
Freefall to Desire
Taste of Desire

KAYLA PERRIN

has been writing since the age of thirteen and once entertained the idea of becoming a teacher. Instead, she has become a *USA TODAY* and *Essence* bestselling author of dozens of mainstream and romance novels, and has been recognized for her talent, including twice winning Romance Writers of America's Top Ten Favorite Books of the Year Award. She has also won a Career Achievement Award for multicultural romance from *RT Book Reviews*. Kayla lives with her daughter in Ontario, Canada. Visit Kayla at www.KaylaPerrin.com.

Taste
OF
DESIRE

Kayla Perrin

KIMANI
ROMANCE

This book is for my father, Lenworth.
You were always a hard worker,
a man of the highest integrity,
and one our family could always rely on.
In short, you are the best father a girl could ask for.
I love you today, tomorrow, and always.

KIMANI PRESS™

ISBN-13: 978-0-373-86224-5

Recycling programs for this product may not exist in your area.

TASTE OF DESIRE

Copyright © 2011 by Kayla Perrin

All rights reserved. The reproduction, transmission or utilization of this work in whole or in part in any form by any electronic, mechanical or other means, now known or hereafter invented, including xerography, photocopying and recording, or in any information storage or retrieval system, is forbidden without written permission. For permission please contact Kimani Press, 225 Duncan Mill Road, Toronto, Ontario M3B 3K9, Canada.

This is a work of fiction. Names, characters, places and incidents are either the product of the author's imagination or are used fictitiously, and any resemblance to actual persons, living or dead, business establishments, events or locales is entirely coincidental.

® and TM are trademarks. Trademarks indicated with ® are registered in the United States Patent and Trademark Office, the Canadian Trade Marks Office and/or other countries.

www.kimanipress.com

Printed in U.S.A.

Dear Reader,

What is your passion? Do you love knitting? Painting landscapes? And is your passion something everyone knows about, or a well-guarded secret?

From childhood, my passion was crafting stories. They say, do what you love, and the rest will follow. That's what I did, and turned my passion into a career.

Salina, my heroine, has a culinary passion. Offered a shortcut to becoming a chef, she soon learns that this offer comes with a price—one she won't pay.

People often put their love lives on the back burner when pursuing their goals, and Salina and Jake are no different. But for them, love is the silver lining after some awful events—if only they'll embrace it.

I hope that whatever your passion is, you're fitting it into your life. But my greater hope is that you don't put love on the back burner. Because that's the greatest passion of all.

Happy reading!

Kayla

Chapter 1

Salina Brown knew well and good that you should always trust your instincts, and indeed she had done that through her entire twenty-seven years. She was smart enough to know that if your gut said something was wrong, you should pay attention. And yet this time, she had ignored her gut, told herself that there was no way the legendary Donald Martin would do anything out of line.

Even before she got on the train in Brooklyn and headed to the Upper East Side for what Donald Martin had said would be "the opportunity of a lifetime," Salina had had a niggling doubt, the odd sensation that perhaps things weren't as Donald said they were.

But he was the expert chef with an endless list of clients. Who was she to question if someone had hired him to prepare a special dinner at a private residence? The Upper East Side address made it clear that whoever had hired Donald had money, and didn't wealthy people love to host dinner parties at their lavish residences? Especially during the holiday season. Despite her reservations, Salina had no doubt that Donald catered such private dinners all the time, and for him to offer her the chance to work with him tonight… well, how lucky was she?

That was the thought Salina concentrated on as she headed to the address where she would be helping Donald to cater the dinner. That and the fact that she would be gaining invaluable private contacts, the kind that would only help her own business grow one day.

Two months earlier, she had been lucky enough to meet the legendary chef at a charity event her sister's law firm had been involved in. And wonder of all wonders, after talking to him, he had offered her the chance to work with him. It had been a dream come true for Salina, whose latest passion was to become a chef. Being able to apprentice with one of New York's greats in the business would surely help fast-track her own path to becoming a chef with her own restaurant one day.

Salina glanced up at the mid-rise condo building overlooking Central Park, her heart beating a little faster. She was nervous, she realized. Nervous about doing her best and proving to Donald—and to herself—that she had what it took to succeed in the competitive world of professional chefs.

Salina approached the beautiful old building, where the immaculately dressed doorman greeted her with a smile and opened the door for her. Inside the building's foyer, the concierge asked her who she was here to see, and she told him what Donald had instructed her to say—that she was his guest.

"Ah, yes. Mr. Martin told me to expect you."

Salina had never been greeted by a doorman back in her native Buffalo, and not in the Brooklyn neighborhood where she lived with her sister. Of course, she had seen exactly this on television and in the movies, and she couldn't help thinking that this was a taste of what her own life would be one day. That by following her passion, she would be able to live at this kind of exclusive address.

Not that she needed all the frills of a lavish lifestyle. Rather, she believed that by following her passion success would come. Every person she admired whose story she had heard or read, all said the same thing. That while not necessarily seeking monetary success, it came when they followed their heart's passion, and Salina was determined that she would be no different.

Indeed, it was why she was here, wasn't it?

"I'll let Mr. Martin know that you're on the way up," the concierge said pleasantly.

Salina nodded and then headed toward the elevators. Soon she was on her way up to the penthouse floor. By the time she was glancing down the hallway to determine in which direction she was supposed to head, she saw a door at the end of the hallway on the right open up. Donald appeared, smiling widely, and gestured to her to come.

Salina made her way down the hallway to him, loosening her scarf as she did. There was no snow outside, but it was frigid, and she was glad she'd thought to wear a scarf to help protect her face from the cold.

"Hello, Donald," Salina said as she reached him.

"Good evening," Donald responded, and held the door open wide for her to enter. As Salina stepped into the apartment's foyer, he added, "Let me take your coat."

Salina gazed around the immaculate residence. While the building itself was a prewar establishment, this unit had been renovated to reflect the design style of the 21st century. Sleek, white leather sofas, polished mahogany hardwood floors and modern art on the walls—the place could easily be featured in a home décor magazine.

"Did you have any trouble finding the place?"

"None," Salina said. "Your directions were perfect."

"Good." Donald took Salina's coat and hung it on the nearby coatrack. As he did, something suddenly struck her as peculiar.

There were no other coats on the rack except for one.

"Where is everyone?" Salina asked. "Or are the residents not arriving until we have the cooking complete?"

"Follow me," was Donald's reply.

Salina frowned. That wasn't the response she had expected. In fact, she suddenly got that odd feeling again. The one that said something wasn't right.

Because if she had come here to help with the cooking, then why did she smell the aroma of food? And not just any food, but Donald's famous spicy curry chicken—the very meal she had told him was her favorite.

Salina's feeling intensified when she followed Donald around the corner toward the dining room and saw that the table was set with two place settings. A bottle of wine sat in a carafe between the table's head spot and the one to its immediate right.

Donald stopped walking and turned to face her. As if he had sensed the direction of her thoughts, he said, "I prepared the meal you said was your favorite. This one *is* your favorite, isn't it?"

Salina knew that what she was about to ask was somewhat silly, because her mind already understood what was going on—even if her heart wanted to deny it. "Didn't you want my help in doing the cooking?"

"Ah, yes. I did tell you that I wanted you here to help me prepare a meal." Donald smiled devilishly. "I admit, I told you a little white lie."

"A little white lie?" Salina asked, her tone implying she was still in the dark.

"There are two place settings here," Donald said, gesturing to the table. "One for me. And one for you."

"B-but—what about the guests? What about the dinner party?"

Now Donald chuckled softly. "That was the little white lie. You're the only one I'm expecting."

"Th—this is *your* place?"

"Yes."

He had lied to her, told her he needed help in catering a Christmas party. All because he wanted to get her here for a romantic evening?

"I wanted to spend some time with you," Donald went on. "Alone."

Salina looked at him as if he had grown two extra heads. "Why would you want to spend time alone with me?" Again, she was aware that she sounded silly, or perhaps that she was playing dense. But she simply didn't understand why Donald would invite her here for this kind of romantic dinner, to spend time alone with him, as he had said. "For God's sake, you're married."

"My wife wanted to escape to Barbados with the kids before Christmas," Donald told her, no discernable reaction at all to the fact that Salina had just mentioned his wife.

And then, without warning, Donald walked toward her and slipped an arm around her waist. He pulled her against him. "Come on," he whispered. "You know what's going on."

She wriggled herself free from his arms and stepped backward, away from him. "No, I don't. I don't understand this at all. Not one bit."

"I've prepared a special dinner for a very special lady." He took a step toward her and Salina instinctively took a step backward. Donald chuckled softly. "What's the problem? You don't like my grand gesture?"

"Are you for real?" Salina asked. "Are you seriously pretending that the issue here isn't that you're *married?*"

"My marriage is none of your concern."

"None of my concern?" Salina shot back. Was the man that foolish? Was he so completely arrogant that he thought she shouldn't care that he had a wife and kids?

"Let me rephrase that. My marriage…it's essentially over. It's been dying for a long time. And ever since I met you… well, I knew we could have something special. Yes, I was hard on you in the beginning. I'm sure you remember. I was fighting my attraction for you. But then it all became so clear to me. Why fight it? I met you by chance, was extremely attracted to you, and then it turned out that your desire was to become a chef. I saw that as destiny." Donald paused. "Our destiny. You and I, Salina, we can be a team."

Salina was flabbergasted. She couldn't even believe what she was hearing. "I don't know what you were thinking, but I do *not* get involved with married men. I don't know what you expected of me, and I'm sorry if you believe that I somehow led you on."

That wasn't what she believed, not in the least. She had simply worked hard for a man who, at first, had been incredibly demanding. She'd believed that he'd been testing her, making sure that she had what it took to work in the competitive culinary business. The tougher he was on her, the harder she had worked because she'd wanted to impress him, show him that he hadn't been wrong in taking her on as an apprentice. That meant working late into the night and not arguing when Donald expected her to be back at his busy midtown Caribbean restaurant the next morning.

But Salina would say what she felt was necessary at this moment, including taking the blame for his error in judgment, because the bigger goal was that she get out of the apartment without incident. She suddenly had no clue what Donald was capable of.

And she also didn't want to make an enemy of him. No, she would never be able to work for him again. But the New York culinary scene was relatively small. And Donald was famous. If he bad-mouthed her because she rejected his advances, that would be a hindrance to her achieving her goal of becoming a chef.

Donald moved toward her swiftly and once again drew her into his arms. "I already explained to you that my marriage is basically over. It's you I want."

And then he planted his mouth on hers and kissed her.

For one stunned moment, Salina couldn't move. But then she sprang into action and fought Donald off her with all of her might. She was disgusted with him, more disgusted than she had ever been with anyone, and she wondered how it was that she had not seen his true nature before now.

Or maybe she had. After his initial coldness—relentless with his demands and coming off as a bit of a jerk—he had suddenly changed. Smiles and winks replaced his scowls. And there were little touches that she always found a bit too friendly…like the ones on her arm or upper back. And sometimes she'd catch him looking at her in a way that had her feeling distinctly uneasy.

But Salina had written it all off as harmless. Since he worked all day in a busy kitchen, she simply believed that he was the type of man who flirted as a way to ease the tension.

It was very clear now just how wrong she was.

Free of his embrace, Donald shot her a gaze of utter disbelief. Disbelief that soon turned to anger. He seemed unable to accept the fact that she was actually rejecting him.

"You'd better consider the consequences of your decision.

Because if you leave now, you'll never work in the restaurant business again."

And just like that, Salina knew that Donald would be the type of man who would be ruthless in his vengeance. He did not like to be rejected, and it was clear he would make her suffer for it. The fact that he would even want to continue with the dinner and whatever else he had planned if she caved to his threats spoke volumes about his unsavory character.

"If that's the way it has to be," Salina said firmly, "then that's the way it has to be. I've never slept with anyone to get anything, and I've never been afraid of hard work. If you can't respect me for that, that's fine. If my life is going to be a little more difficult in terms of achieving my goal because I won't sleep with you, then so be it. But I am about to walk out that door right now, and if you touch me—I swear to God I will scream so loud everyone in this building will come running to see what's wrong. And then I'll press charges against you for sexual harassment. So don't you dare think you can threaten me."

Salina wasn't sure where she got strength to stand up to Donald like that. Perhaps it was the fact that she knew that if she stayed in his apartment with him and tried to play nice, it would end badly for her. Playing nice with a man like Donald Martin, whose ego was clearly larger than the state of New York, would only lead to more problems. She had to be firm, had to get out of the apartment immediately.

Donald was clearly shocked by her words, and Salina could see the anger on his face, but he made no move to walk toward her as she stepped backward one foot at a time, her eyes watching him carefully. When she reached the living room she turned and hustled to the foyer, where she grabbed her coat and scarf from the coatrack. She didn't look back as she scrambled out the door.

Salina left the apartment, running. She ran straight for the nearest exit sign instead of the elevator, and ran down sixteen flights on pure adrenaline.

She was aware of the odd looks she got from the concierge and then the doorman, but she didn't care. She wanted to get as far away from this upscale New York address as possible.

She was humiliated. As she slowed to a fast walk instead of a jog, Salina asked herself if she had done something to let Donald think that she would be the type of woman who would sleep her way to the top.

Seeing the subway sign, she almost cried with relief. To her, the sign must have been like what a buoy would be to a person drowning in deep water.

She made her way down the stairs, contemplating the question she had asked herself. No, she decided. She had not portrayed herself as a woman who would barter sex for success. She was *not* going to take the blame for Donald's bad behavior.

Perhaps she should have been firmer with him before. When he'd started with the little smiles and touches, maybe she should have made it clear to him that he was crossing the lines of professional conduct.

But it was too late now to change the past. All Salina could do was move forward.

And as she got onto the subway car and sank into a seat in the corner, all she could wonder was how something that had started with such promise could go so terribly wrong.

But what had happened in Donald's penthouse suite proved the adage true: that if something seemed too good to be true, then it was.

Donald Martin may have been one of the best chefs in New York city, but the price to learn the ropes from him had proved too steep.

The opportunity of a lifetime, gone in an instant.

God help her, how would Salina ever accomplish her dream now?

Chapter 2

Three weeks later Salina was still in the dumps over what had happened with Donald Martin. She had applied at many more restaurants, hoping that she would have some success in landing another apprenticeship position. She had anything but. She didn't know if Donald had bad-mouthed her in any way, but suspected that he hadn't. Indeed, if he was smart, he wouldn't. He had to know that if he did anything to hinder her opportunities for employment, she could easily let the world know about his failed seduction plan. And given the fact that he knew Salina's sister was a lawyer—one who specialized in civil litigation—the thought must have come to him that Salina would slap him with a lawsuit if he tried to mess with her possible future employment in any way.

No, Salina believed that prospects were grim because the economic downturn had affected many restaurants to the point where they weren't taking on any new employees. What that meant for her was that she was going to have to go back to her original plan—go to culinary school in order to see her dream fulfilled. And after the experience she had with Donald, she valued the idea of taking the regular route to success, as opposed to the shortcut. That said, the regular route was going to take her years and thousands of dollars. Thousands of dollars for culinary school that she didn't have.

She had two options. Either she could head back to Buffalo and once again work in day care, or she was going to have to find something else to do in the city. She was loving the vibe of New York and wanted to stay. But she needed to stand on her own two feet and not live off her sister.

There was another reason she didn't want to head back to Buffalo. All her friends and family there had had such high hopes for her when she told them she was heading to New York to work as a chef. She didn't want to go back to her hometown with her tail between her legs, as the saying went, because that would be admitting she had failed.

She was at home on Thursday evening looking through the classifieds and trying to see what other positions might be available when her sister came in the door and practically sang, "I have the perfect opportunity for you."

"What kind of opportunity?" Salina asked.

"The kind that means cash," Emma replied, smiling brightly. She wore her hair short, the style Halle Berry had made famous, with bangs falling over her forehead. It was a professional look, easy to maintain and suited Emma's face very well.

Salina narrowed her eyes as she stared at her sister. "Ah, I get it. You want me to start pulling my weight around here," she joked.

"You know you're welcome to stay here as long as you want or need," Emma told her. She approached the table where Salina was sitting, and placed her briefcase on it. "Seriously, though. I think I have the answer for your job woes. At least for a little while."

Salina put down the paper she had been reading, feeling hopeful for the first time in three weeks. "You got me an interview for a job? What kind of job?" The answer came to her a moment later. "Oh, I know. The receptionist at your law firm finally quit, didn't she?"

Salina wasn't sure she wanted to do reception work, as it wasn't the kind of job that would advance her particular career interest. But the truth was, she was at a point where she had to acknowledge that beggars couldn't be choosers. She would do what she had to in order to accomplish her bigger goal.

And that goal was to fund her way through culinary school.

"No, not a receptionist." Emma began to unbutton her coat. "It's in a field you've worked in before—well, sort of—so I think it's right up your alley."

Salina narrowed her eyes at her sister. "I'm confused."

"Of course you're confused. How many job avenues have you followed?"

Emma smiled wryly, and Salina had to concede that her sister had a point. It was true that she had, in her short twenty-seven years, contemplated about four major career paths. She had become a lifeguard at seventeen, and thought for sure she would end up working in that field for a very long time. Not simply as a lifeguard, but in management at a recreation center. She enjoyed working with children, and especially enjoyed the summer programs where she had helped inner-city kids learn how to swim.

Her love of working with children had led her to her second career path: working in day care. She had done so for four years, hoping to one day have her own child-care company. However, she found that she got too attached to the little darlings in the day care, and when they left to go to school, or because their parents moved, Salina had always been deeply saddened. She realized just how easy it was to get attached to children, and that had her rethinking her career choice.

She had gone on a totally different career path after that, applying to get onto the police force. Again, she'd been interested in doing a job where she could help people and be a positive role model, and she felt she could do that as a police officer in the city of Buffalo. She had gone through the initial physical training and study—and then realized that law enforcement wasn't for her.

Just six months ago she had decided to pursue her latest passion: cooking. All her life she had liked to cook, to make meals and desserts for family and friends. After hearing a radio show where a woman had talked about how people should turn their passion into a career, the proverbial lightbulb had turned on in her brain. She loved to cook. She should become a chef.

Salina had done her research and learned that it would cost a small fortune to go to a respected culinary school. But there were other ways to achieve her dream. If she could be hired as an apprentice, she could learn the ropes from a master and gain the skills necessary to become a chef and open her own restaurant one day.

"Can't guess?" Emma asked.

"Well, I know it's not going to be police work," Salina said, smiling sweetly. "Is there a community pool that needs a lifeguard?"

"I've gotten you a job as a nanny," Emma told her, since she clearly couldn't guess.

"A nanny?" Salina asked. "I've never been a nanny."

"That's why I said that it was *sort of* in a field you've worked in before. A colleague at my law firm needs someone immediately. His nanny had to go to Mexico for a family emergency, and he's left in a bind. He needs someone right away."

"But I've never been a nanny," Salina repeated.

"But you've worked in day care. You worked in day care for four years. That's a long time, and that's relevant experience."

Salina frowned, but realized that her sister was right. She *did* have experience, and she *could* work as a nanny, even if she hadn't officially done so in the past. "Who needs the nanny? Is it someone I met before?"

"Jake McKnight," Emma replied. "And yes, you met him."

Even before Emma said that Salina had met him, a vivid image of Jake McKnight came into Salina's mind. She had met him at the same charity event where she'd met Donald Martin, albeit briefly.

What Salina remembered was that he was a very attractive man, and one who had stayed at the charity event for a very short time. Initially, upon meeting him and shaking his hand, Salina's interest had been piqued. In fact, she had been surprised at her instant interest in Jake McKnight. Perhaps because it had been such a long time since she had been involved with anyone—the last guy being an aspiring musician she had met at a friend's party in Buffalo—she had been particularly susceptible to an attractive face, not to mention a body that was clearly fine. But after that initial handshake, Jake turned away from her and greeted the next person, and so on. As Salina had watched him, she had come to the conclusion that he was the brooding sort. He hadn't been smiling, but he had made the rounds at the event, greeting everyone, and then he quickly left. Salina had gotten the impression that he was not the kind of guy who liked to socialize.

"I met him at that charity event," Salina said.

"That's right," Emma said. "Jake's a really nice guy, and had the misfortune of losing his wife two years ago. It was a tragic accident. Slippery roads, and her car skidded off the highway into a ditch, hitting a tree. Jake was devastated."

"Oh, how awful!" Salina said. Now she understood why he was brooding. To lose someone you loved so unexpectedly and in such a horrible way, had to be absolutely heartbreaking.

"Like I said, he's in a bind," Emma explained. "His nanny is from Mexico, and apparently her mother is gravely ill. She had to leave immediately, and with Jake being a single parent, he needs help. He can't very well bring his daughter to the office every day. He had to today though, which is how I got to know about his issue. I told him that you were looking for work and that you had extensive experience in day care. He was immediately interested. This will be a win-win situation. A good temporary job for you, and a lifesaver for him."

Salina was relieved to hear the word *temporary*. As much as she had enjoyed working in day care, despite the emotional downfalls, she didn't want a career in child care anymore. She loved kids, but her goal was to become a chef.

"How temporary?" Salina asked.

"Probably two weeks," Emma said. "That's what he said. His nanny got on a plane two days ago. I get the sense that she's going to be in touch with him to let him know exactly how much time she needs, but two weeks was her best guess. He did say that her mother was gravely ill, so if she passes away, who knows? I suspect it could be anywhere from two weeks to four, depending on how much time Maria might want to spend with family dealing with funeral arrangements and so forth, if it comes to that."

Salina considered her sister's proposition. "I agree that

this might be a great temporary job for me, but what if I get a call about permanent employment?"

"You can cross that bridge when you get to it," Emma told her. "Probably within the time that it would take for Maria to go to Mexico and return, you wouldn't be starting your new position yet. And if you don't get a job in the meantime, at least you'll have some income."

Salina nodded, but she wasn't entirely convinced. "How old is his child?"

"He has a little girl, and she's four. From what I witnessed of her in the office, she is very well behaved."

"Four. That's such a darling age," Salina commented. The problem however, was that with four-year-olds—cute as a button and typically loads of fun—you got attached to them more easily. At least, Salina always had.

"You're going to do it, right?" Emma asked.

Did Salina really have any other choice? She would be helping out her sister's colleague and herself in the process. "I—I guess."

"You don't sound excited," Emma commented.

"It's not exactly what I had in mind in terms of employment, but like you say, I've had some experience in day care, so I'm sure I can do an adequate job. And as long as it's only temporary, and I don't have to worry about my true career goal being derailed." And if this job helped to put extra money in her pocket so that she could fund culinary school, all the better.

"Great," Emma said. "I told Jake you would call him this evening, arrange to meet him immediately."

"What?"

"I told you, he's urgently in need of someone. There's no time to waste."

"Where does he live?"

"He's in Manhattan," Emma explained. "Actually, United Nations Plaza. The Trump World Tower residences there."

"That's a nice address," Salina said. And even though she knew she shouldn't, she couldn't help thinking about Donald Martin, a man with money who had felt that he was entitled to something extra from her. Salina didn't like the idea of possibly meeting another wealthy man who had expectations of something on the side for his pleasure.

"Don't worry," Emma said, and Salina knew that her sister had read her thoughts. They were close that way, and could often gauge what each other was thinking. "Jake is a true gentleman, and in fact, he hasn't even dated since his wife's death. He has totally thrown himself into work. Jake's not going to do anything crazy."

Salina nodded. "Course not. You know him, and you wouldn't recommend me for the job if you thought there was anything untoward about him. I just couldn't help thinking about Donald for a moment. I guess that I may be a little jaded."

"I know," Emma said. "And I told you that you totally need to slap Donald's behind with a lawsuit. What he did to you was out of line and unconscionable."

Salina raised her hand. "I know, but a lawsuit would be emotionally taxing, and mean that I have to see him in court, not to mention spend money that I don't have."

"I wouldn't charge you," Emma said. "You know I would do it for the satisfaction of seeing a jerk like him go down."

"Well, there would have to be *some* cost. Court costs, I don't know. The bottom line is, the most important cost to me would be the emotional one. And I'm not willing to pay it." Salina spoke firmly, hoping to put an end to this discussion once and for all. She knew her sister loved her and had her best interests at heart, but the idea of justice for her was not the same as Emma's thoughts on justice.

To turn the conversation away from the ugly experience she only wanted to forget, Salina said, "So, you want me to call Jake now?"

"Yes, that would be great. I told him to expect your call." Emma smiled sheepishly, the look saying that she knew her sister would have said yes to the deal all along.

"All right, give me his number."

Emma rattled off the phone number, and then explained that Jake should be at home because he had left work early with his daughter.

"I'll call him right away."

Salina went to the bedroom to make the call in private, and a minute later she had Jake on the line. "Hello, Mr. Mc-Knight?"

"You must be Emma's sister," he said without preamble. "Salina?"

"Yes," Salina answered. She couldn't help noting that the man's voice was deep and sexy.

"Please, call me Jake."

"Okay. Hi, Jake. I understand you need a temporary nanny."

"Yes. Can you start immediately?"

Salina had not expected that Mr. McKnight would want her to start immediately. She figured he might even be interviewing other prospects to feel one hundred percent comfortable with his decision. But she said, "Absolutely. If you want me to start right away, I can."

"By right away, I mean right now. If you could come to my home, meet with me and meet with my daughter, that would make things much easier for when you officially start tomorrow morning."

"You want me to come right now?" Salina asked, glancing at the clock. It was shortly after 6:00 p.m.

"Is that a problem?"

"No. No problem at all. Just tell me your address, and I'll be on my way."

As Salina scribbled the information on a pad, the image of Jake's handsome face popped into her mind. Releasing a sigh, she vowed to resist the temptation of his allure and promised herself to keep the assignment professional.

Chapter 3

An hour later Salina had exited the subway and was heading to Trump World Tower. The building was enormous, its black-and-bronze-tinted glass stunning. Across the street was a park with landscaped grounds and fountains, which Salina could only imagine was incredibly beautiful in the spring and summer. The Trump building towered over the neighboring United Nations Plaza Tower, a structure with a unique design that angled inward as it neared the top, to form a pointed peak. Both addresses were high-priced real estate, and Salina couldn't help remembering that unfortunate day weeks ago as she headed toward the exclusive residence on the Upper East Side, but she swallowed her nervousness and reminded herself that Jake McKnight, devoted father and widow, was not Donald Martin.

She went through the typical doorman greeting, followed by the concierge calling her up to Mr. McKnight's suite. Within minutes, she was on her way up the elevator to the fifty-sixth floor.

A few minutes later she was knocking on door 56-B. Within seconds Jake opened the door.

And even though Salina had known he was very attractive, she was taken aback by the sight of him.

The man was gorgeous. She had forgotten just how much so. He was tall, definitely over six feet. He had wide shoulders, the kind that said he worked out or had played sports. He was clean-shaven, making his strong jawline clearly evident. His golden brown skin was similar in complexion to hers. Everything about him was utterly sexy, but his eyes were his most compelling feature—brown with flecks of gold.

"Hello," Jake said.

"Hi," Salina responded. And she noticed in Jake's eyes the same expression she had seen the night of the charity event. Then, she had thought he was simply brooding. Now she recognized the look for what it was—sadness.

"Thanks for coming right away," Jake said.

"No problem. I'm happy to help out."

"Come in."

Jake stepped backward so that she could enter the apartment, and Salina did so, looking around as she did. The first thing she noticed was the high ceiling, probably around ten feet. The living room area was large, with polished oak floors. Salina guessed that this space alone was probably twelve hundred square feet or so. The unit boasted floor-to-ceiling windows with an incredible view of the New York skyline. Though it was dark outside, Salina could see the Chrysler building in the distance.

Jake's furnishings were tasteful and elegant. A sandy-beige-colored sectional was near one window in the living room, which looked soft and comfortable. A matching recliner was opposite that sofa close to one of the walls. On the main wall facing the large sectional was a giant plasma television, likely sixty inches.

Unlike Donald's residence, this condo didn't feel sterile. It felt homey. In fact, there were toys scattered over the floor in front of the sectional—little horse figurines and stuffed animals. And as Salina walked farther into the living room, she could see that there was a little girl sleeping peacefully on the sofa, a knit blanket wrapped over her small frame.

"Oh, my goodness, she's adorable," Salina couldn't help exclaiming. And she was. The little girl's hair was done in two pigtails, and she had one of the cutest little faces Salina had ever seen. Round, like a cherub. She looked like a little angel.

"Thank you," Jake said, a smile touching his lips. Then he faced Salina once more. "I realize that we never talked about a price. I just offered you the job and you accepted. But rest assured, the salary I'm offering is going to be well worth your time."

And then Jake told her a figure, and Salina was flabbergasted. It was more than she had expected. At least double what she thought he might offer—and very generous.

"Will that be okay?" Jake asked.

"Okay? That's more than okay. In fact, it's quite generous. Thank you."

"No. Thank *you*. You are really helping me out here."

"What time do you expect me to arrive for work?"

"I know you're in Brooklyn, and really what I need is someone to be here in the mornings with Riquet, and get her up, get her dressed for preschool. At noon, she needs to be picked up from her preschool, and you would take care of her in the afternoon. She has a number of activities she's involved in, like her art class, ballet, piano lessons and gymnastics. Four days of the week, she has something to do in the afternoons. That also includes scheduled play dates.

Maria has the schedule set, which I'll show you." He paused. "I know this is sudden, but you'll have a pretty demanding schedule, so I was thinking that, with you living in Brooklyn, it'd be better if you lived here for the time being."

Salina swallowed. "You want me to live here?"

"Ideally, yes. I'd love for you to be a live-in nanny, like Maria was. Like Maria *is*," he corrected. "I think it will be much simpler that way."

Salina hadn't considered that the position would be live-in, but it made sense, given the fact that she didn't live down the street from him. The commute every morning on a crowded subway would be stressful and annoying.

She said, "I understand."

"If you're not comfortable with that, then by all means you can feel free to come in each day. That said, your job will begin at six-thirty in the morning. I think it would be easier for you if you were right here on the premises and didn't have to add extra time to your day by coming and going."

"Yes, that makes sense." Salina paused, crossed her arms over her chest. "I feel I should disclose something here—in case it's a concern to you. I've never been a nanny before. I've only worked in day care."

"Well, your sister speaks very highly of you. I trust her opinion and her judgment. If she says you'd be a great nanny, I believe her."

Salina nodded. "I appreciate that."

"I'm the one who's grateful." He paused briefly. "Let me show you your bedroom. Whether or not you decide to commute each day, you can use this bedroom as your private space while you're here."

"Okay."

Salina followed Jake to the right, to the hallway that led to two bedrooms. On the wall, she noticed a series of portraits of Jake, a toddler and a beautiful dark-skinned woman with shoulder-length hair and a warm, earnest smile.

Jake's late wife.

"Right here," Jake said.

At the sound of his voice, Salina hustled forward to the bedroom door he had just opened. As she walked into the room, she was pleasantly surprised at what she saw. The bedroom was a decent size, with an oak four-poster bed decorated to a woman's sensibilities. There was a desk in the room, as well as a recliner in the corner beside the window. This window also went from the ceiling to the floor. Salina walked toward it and looked outside. She smiled at the sight of the East River.

Turning to Jake, she said, "Your condo has amazing views."

"It's a beautiful location. The views are priceless."

"I couldn't agree more."

"This is the bedroom where Maria sleeps," Jake explained. "Should you decide to live in while you're working for me, this is where you'll sleep, as well."

Salina nodded.

"You probably have friends you hang out with, and maybe you're dating. Once Riquet is in bed, you're free for the evening, and you can head out and do whatever you like. I usually work late, but on occasion I get home around six, so if you have particular plans or want to head out to shop, eat or simply have some downtime, you're free to do that."

"Right," Salina said.

"You'll find there's room in the closet for your clothes should you decide to live here for the next two weeks, and there's also a bathroom off this bedroom that you would have all to yourself."

"Excellent." One of Salina's reservations over the idea of living here while working for Jake was the idea that she

Taste of Desire

might not have enough personal space during her off hours. But the condo was large and had enough room for her to have a space to call her own.

"I think I heard Riquet," Jake said suddenly, and walked past Salina out of the bedroom. As he passed her, she got a whiff of his cologne. It was a musky scent that flirted with her nostrils.

Salina wrapped her arms around her torso as she slowly walked behind Jake. Her eyes lowered to his jeans—and his butt. As behinds went, it was certainly a cute one.

And then she felt guilty. Why was she checking him out? The answer came to her immediately. He was gorgeous. Of course she couldn't help noticing how fine the man was.

Salina wondered why a man as attractive as Jake was still single. In a city like this where eligible bachelors were few, why had another woman not snagged him? A lot of men who were suddenly left with a small child to raise would have tried to find a new partner, if only to give the child a mother figure. The fact that Jake was still single must mean that he wasn't ready for a new relationship.

Why am I even wondering about Jake and whether or not he's ready for a relationship? Seriously, Salina, how inappropriate is that?

Jake, who had disappeared into the living room, looked in Salina's direction once she got there. "Ready to meet your new charge?" he asked.

"Absolutely." Salina walked farther into the living room, approaching Riquet slowly. "Hello."

"Hi," Riquet said guardedly. She was looking at Salina with suspicion.

"You remember I told you that someone else would be coming to work as a nanny for a little while until Maria comes back?" Jake said.

The girl nodded, keeping her eyes on Salina.

"Well, sweetheart. This is her."

"My name is Salina," Salina said gently. She took a seat on the sofa near Riquet's feet. "What's your name?"

"Riquet," Riquet answered. "It's French."

"It's a very pretty name." Salina glanced to the left at the papers scattered on the coffee table. "Did you draw that picture?" Salina asked. "The one of the horse? Because it's beautiful." She was complimenting Riquet as a way to hopefully have the girl warm to her. This poor darling had suffered a lot in her young life, having lost her mother. Now, with her regular nanny gone, she might feel confused, distressed and afraid.

Riquet nodded. "Yes, I did."

"You're very talented," Salina said, smiling. Which wasn't a lie. The artwork displayed a lot of promise for a girl so young. Other four-year-olds were drawing stick figures or scribbling, but Riquet's art showed dimension and depth. Salina was certain she was a budding artist.

Riquet sat up, smiling, too. "I love horses," she said. "I love to draw horses eating food, or running in fields, or anywhere. Did you know I rode on a horse before?"

"It was a pony in Central Park," Jake said.

"Daddy, it was a horse," Riquet insisted. Then she rolled her eyes, as if to say he simply didn't understand.

Looking at Jake, Salina saw him bite back a smile.

"You know, honey—you're right. It was a horse. I forgot."

"It was a small horse, but it was still a horse," Riquet went on. Then she looked at Salina again. "Do you like horses?"

"I love horses," Salina told her.

"My mommy used to love horses, too," Riquet said sadly. "She's in heaven now."

"I know." Salina sighed softly. "I'm so sorry she's not with you anymore."

"Daddy said she had a more important job to do in heaven.

She's an angel now, and she watches over me and daddy, to make sure we're safe." The little girl smiled broadly.

The words tugged at Salina's heartstrings. Such bravery for a girl so young.

"I saw her picture," Salina said. "She was very beautiful."

"She's the most beautiful angel in heaven. My daddy says that all the time."

Hearing Riquet speak made it clear to Salina that Jake McKnight was a man of honor. It was obvious he had loved his wife dearly, and in her absence he had tried to share with his daughter all the wonderful things about the woman. In this day and age, when happily-ever-after stories were tainted by the reality of infidelity and divorce, Salina admired the fact that Jake had truly loved his wife.

"Can I show you my bedroom?" Riquet asked.

"You want to show me your bedroom?" Salina asked.

Riquet nodded vigorously. "I have lots of horses in there."

Salina stood and extended her hand to the girl. "Sure."

A smile spread on Jake's face as he watched Riquet walk off toward her bedroom with Salina. He was impressed. Salina had instantly taken to his daughter. Indeed, Riquet had also instantly taken to Salina in a way he had never known her to so immediately like or trust anyone else.

It did his heart good to know that he had made the right choice. Thank goodness for Emma letting him know that her sister was not only in need of work, but that she had worked with children before. It was clear Salina was a natural. She obviously loved children, and would be a great replacement for Maria while she was gone.

He heard laughter, airy and bright, as he approached Riquet's bedroom. Salina's and Riquet's. It had been a long time since he'd heard laughter like that between these walls, the kind that filled the apartment with warmth.

Emma had told him that Salina was twenty-seven, which meant she was a good twenty years younger than Maria. Maria had brought a wealth of experience to her position as nanny, having raised two children single-handedly. Those children were now attending NYU, her daughter studying to be a future filmmaker, and her son in a pre-med program. Maria was a gentle and loving woman, and had been a good replacement caregiver in the wake of his wife, Janine's, death.

From everything Emma had said—and from what Jake was witnessing now—Salina would also be an equally good replacement. He could tell that she was a free spirit, unlike Maria, who was more serious, and she would no doubt do well with Riquet. He only hoped that with her younger age she wouldn't be obsessed with partying every night, or gabbing on the phone with her friends at all hours. That had been the problem with the first nanny Jake had hired, a twenty-two-year-old au pair from England.

But he had known Emma for five years, and he trusted her. Indeed, if Salina was anything like her sister, she would be an extremely hard worker.

Salina and Riquet exited the bedroom, the two holding hands. This was working out better than he had expected. Here he had worried that Riquet would not take well to Maria's replacement, but he needn't have been concerned.

Salina met his gaze, her lips parted in a smile, and Jake was instantly struck by her beauty. She had big, bright eyes, a slender and shapely frame, and full lips that made him think of kissing. Indeed, he felt a pull of attraction so strong for her in that moment it stunned him. He opened his mouth to speak, but found he had to swallow first.

"Um," he said, but no other words came to his lips.

"Riquet's bedroom is gorgeous," Salina announced. "And

all those pictures of hers on the wall... My goodness, she's a talented little artist."

"Yes." Jake cleared his throat. "Yes, she is."

"Are you sleeping over?" Riquet asked.

"Not tonight, sweetie," Salina said.

Riquet looked up at Salina with doe eyes. "Please?"

"I can't. I don't have anything I need with me."

"Awww." Riquet crossed her arms over her chest.

Jake bent down in front of his daughter. "Don't worry. Salina will be back in the morning before you wake up. She's going to be your nanny while Maria is away, so you'll be seeing her every day. Okay?"

Riquet nodded, accepting Jake's words.

"I'd better go," Salina said. "I've got to head back to Brooklyn, then get back here bright and early."

Jake stood to face her, and once again her lips were parted in a slight smile. Goodness, those lips were sexy, and he couldn't help thinking that they looked utterly kissable.

Jake's chest tightened. What was wrong with him? It wasn't like him to feel this kind of attraction to a pretty face.

He averted his gaze, hoping to break whatever temporary spell he was under.

"Bye, Riquet. See you tomorrow. See you in the morning, Jake."

"Yes, see you in the morning," Jake replied. "Oh—wait."

He hurried to his bedroom and retrieved the extra key. Returning to the foyer a moment later, he passed it to Salina, his fingers brushing against hers as he did.

Damn if he didn't feel an electrical charge.

"I'll let the staff downstairs know your status as my new nanny, so you won't have any problem coming and going. And with this key you can let yourself in to the apartment when you arrive in the morning."

"Thanks."

Jake nodded, still making sure to avoid direct eye contact with Salina.

Once she was out the door, he released a breath he didn't realize he was holding.

He would take a cold shower, and hopefully that would rid his system of whatever had him in its temporary grip.

By the morning he would be back to normal.

He was sure of it.

Chapter 4

"So how did it go?" Emma asked when Salina returned to the apartment, her eyes bright with expectation. "How did you like him?"

"It was great," Salina responded. "Jake seems like a lovely man who really adored his wife. The apartment is still filled with her pictures, memories of the two of them together, and of course of them with their daughter. Riquet is just precious. It broke my heart as she was telling me how her father told her that her mother is in heaven, and that she's one of the most beautiful angels up there." Salina sighed. "I can't imagine that kind of heartbreaking loss. Especially after they couldn't have been married all that long. It's one thing to lose someone after years and years of marriage, but to be left with a small child to raise—"

Salina stopped speaking and inhaled a deep breath. She could already see herself getting attached to Riquet, and she needed to do her best to keep a bit of an emotional distance. She would only be in the girl's life temporarily.

"I assume you'll be starting in the morning," Emma said.

"Yes. I was worried that Riquet might take a while to get used to me, but she really took to me. I'm not sure why, maybe it's just her friendly nature. She's really adorable, and I'm excited about this opportunity."

"Good," Emma said. "I'm glad."

"You said he hasn't dated since his wife's death?" Salina found herself asking.

"No," Emma replied, shaking her head. "Janine was his world. In fact, what I've seen him do more than anything else is throw himself into work even more than he did before."

"Workaholic, hmm?" Salina said. "Isn't that like the pot calling the kettle black?" Maybe people who worked in the legal field had to be workaholics. The devotion to the kind of work they did—which at times could be mind-numbingly boring going through all those case files, as far as Salina was concerned—had to require that a person be totally committed to their vocation.

"I know I'm bad," Emma began, "but Jake's even more of a workaholic than I am. At least I take the weekends off. Zachary would have a fit if I didn't make time for him. He already complains that I don't spend enough time with him as it is. Jake, however, has been known to head into the office on Saturday and work all day. It's obvious to me and everyone else at the firm that that is his way of dealing with the pain."

"He works on Saturdays?"

"Oh, yeah. Quite a bit." Emma paused. "He didn't talk to you about his schedule?"

"Well…not really. I guess I just figured it'd be a Monday-to-Friday gig. That said, he's offering me a very generous salary, so I'm not going to complain."

"This'll be great for you," Emma said.

"And speaking of my new job," Salina began, "I'd better

get to bed. I have to be there bright and early in the morning." She went to her sister and gave her a hug. "Thanks again, and I'll see you tomorrow."

The early morning commute to Manhattan was awful. Not only did the world seem a colder, more miserable place, Salina couldn't help thinking that she could be snug in bed for another hour, instead of up at an ungodly time to head to work. She was glad she'd decided to pack a small suitcase—just in case—because she had a feeling she would end up staying at Jake's place tonight.

When she arrived at Jake's residence, she found that she had no problem gaining entrance to the building, as he'd told her she wouldn't. She made her way up to the fifty-sixth floor, her stomach tickling on the insanely fast ride up the elevator.

She felt a little awkward letting herself into the apartment—as though she should knock first—but it was early, only a little after six, and she didn't want to wake Jake if he wasn't already up.

She opened the door and crept into the apartment. As she stepped into the living room, she was surprised to see Jake sitting at the nearby dining room table.

"Oh," she said, startled. She put down the travel bag she'd brought with her. "I didn't think you'd be up."

He was wearing a T-shirt and black silk pajama bottoms, and looked like he was ready to pose for a high-end photo shoot. How was it that he looked just as good so early in the morning as he had the night before?

"Morning," Jake said, rising. "I wanted to make sure you had all the information you needed for the day." He lifted a black book from the table. "This is Riquet's schedule, with all the pertinent phone numbers you'll need, the address for her preschool and the addresses where she needs to go for her various extracurricular activities."

Salina approached Jake and he handed her the book. The gold-embossed letters engraved into the leather read: "RI-QUET'S CALENDAR."

"It should all be self-explanatory," Jake went on as Salina opened the book and found the appropriate date in January.

Salina continued to flip the pages forward. She could see that Riquet's calendar had been scheduled all the way to March. Even play dates.

"There's a lot in there, but what you'll notice is that the schedule is the same for every week. Today is Wednesday, so after preschool Riquet has a play date from one-thirty to two-thirty with Sarah, and then ballet lessons."

"The play dates are always the same every week? With the same kids?"

"Yes," Jake replied. "Maria believes—and I concur—that having a regular routine for Riquet is the best thing. This way, she'll know what to expect every day and won't feel any anxiety."

Salina nodded, but she didn't totally agree. Routines were necessary, yes. But so was spontaneity. A child needed to learn that there could be a break from routine and that the world wouldn't fall apart. Life didn't always follow the pattern people planned for.

Jake's wife's premature death proved that.

Salina flipped back to today's date on the calendar, and noted that in the lunch column even a meal had been marked in. Macaroni and cheese. Certainly the girl's routine wasn't so rigid that there couldn't be spontaneity when it came to meals?

"Everything should be in there that you need, and if you find you're confused about anything, please don't hesitate to call."

"Got it," Salina said. As she closed the book and looked at Jake, offering him a smile, she noticed that he averted his gaze.

"I'm going to get dressed, get ready for work. Riquet usually wakes up by seven, and on Wednesdays Maria makes her pancakes for breakfast. Her preschool is about a twenty-minute car ride—Ed, my driver, will be downstairs at eight to pick you up."

"We have a driver?"

"Once he gets me to the office by seven-thirty, he heads right back here so he can take Riquet to school. Once she's in her class, he can bring you back to the apartment or out to do shopping, run the necessary errands you need to."

"Okay." Salina nodded. Being a nanny in New York City entailed a lot more than she'd anticipated. Riquet's schedule was busier than she'd known any child's to be back in Buffalo.

"I'm going to shower now," Jake said, still not directly looking her in the eye.

Once Jake headed off in the direction of his bedroom, Salina went to the kitchen. It was large, with a wraparound counter that ended in a breakfast bar. The cupboards were maple, a contrast to the pale beige backsplash and beige-tiled floor.

Coffee was already brewed in an elaborate-looking coffeemaker. Salina would have to ask Jake how to use it.

Though she had time, she went into the cupboard and looked for the items besides eggs she would need to make pancakes. She found flour and sugar, but no vanilla, and sadly no cinnamon. She would make sure that she picked those items up today once Riquet was in school.

Salina spent the next few minutes familiarizing herself with the kitchen. It was a chef's dream. Double ovens, a gas stovetop, large counter space for working… She would enjoy making many a meal here.

She glanced toward the dining room and saw that the only thing on the table was Jake's large coffee mug. There were no plates in the sink. Jake hadn't eaten.

He hadn't said that she should make breakfast for him, and Salina wondered if he planned to pick something up on the way to work. Perhaps a bagel. Something he could eat quickly and go.

Well, that wouldn't do. Jake was already up with files before him, doing work. He needed food for energy and sustenance.

Salina brought her small suitcase to Maria's room and set it on the bed. Then she went back to the kitchen and measured the ingredients to make pancakes. She was finishing the first batch when Jake entered the kitchen.

Freshly showered, the man looked sexy as hell. Salina swallowed. She needed to keep things in perspective. She had to remain professional, and not go all tongue-tied when she saw him. So what if he was a gorgeous man, with his white dress shirt partially unbuttoned and revealing a hint of golden brown skin on his chest, and the scent of his aftershave smelling so incredibly appealing? None of that would affect her performance as nanny.

Salina placed two medium-size pancakes on a plate for Jake, then extended it to him. She already had butter and syrup on the table for him. "You didn't say if I should make breakfast for you, but I took the liberty."

Jake finished buttoning his shirt, then took the plate from Salina. "Normally I eat on the run," he began, "but this is good. Thank you."

Salina glanced at the clock on the microwave's display.

It was almost six forty-five. She took the skillet off the stove and placed it on a back burner, then turned to head toward Riquet's bedroom to check on her. But before she got out of the kitchen, Jake spoke.

"These are delicious," he said.

"You like them?"

"I've never had pancakes this tasty before. And these are fluffy and light…amazing."

Salina beamed. "And I didn't even get to make them the way I normally do—with all the ingredients I typically use."

"They taste better than this?" he asked, his tone saying that was hard to believe.

"Oh, yeah." Salina walked toward him. "When I have all the right ingredients, they're even better."

"Then I might just ask that you make these again tomorrow morning," Jake told her.

Salina noticed that he was looking at her directly in the eye, not avoiding her gaze as he had been earlier.

"Anything you'd like to eat for breakfast, I can make it for you. I make a really great western omelet with turkey instead of ham. Home fries, the whole bit."

"You're a budding chef, are you?"

Salina guessed that Jake was just making an offhanded comment, but she said, "Actually, I am."

"You are?" Jake asked between swallows.

Salina took the liberty of sitting at the table beside him. "Yes. I guess my sister didn't tell you. But that's how I came to be in New York. I thought I would pursue my passion for cooking. Right now I'm trying to save money for culinary school."

"Ahhh. No, Emma didn't tell me. How long have you been cooking?"

Salina shrugged. "As long as I can remember. It's always been a passion of mine. I hope you don't mind if I change some of Riquet's lunch dishes—with her permission, of course."

"Sure. If she doesn't mind, I'm sure she might even enjoy a change of pace."

Salina heard the sound just as Jake looked beyond her. She turned, following the direction of where he was looking. Riquet, holding a stuffed horse, had just walked into the adjacent living room.

Salina rose from her chair and went to greet the little girl. "Good morning, Riquet."

Riquet beamed at her. "Good morning." Then she went to her father and threw her little arms around his chest. "Morning, Daddy."

"Morning, sweetheart," Jake said. "You've got to get ready for preschool now. You be a good girl for Salina, okay?"

"I will."

Salina took Riquet's hand and then walked with her to her bedroom, ready to start her official duties as nanny.

The day with Riquet passed without incident. After Riquet went to her preschool, Salina had Ed, the driver, take her to a market where she could pick up a number of fresh vegetables and fruit. She'd noticed that Jake's place didn't have much fruit, perhaps because Maria hadn't been around to do the shopping.

Salina stuck with the macaroni and cheese for lunch, simply because she didn't have time to prepare anything more elaborate by the time she'd run around doing the shopping. She had added extra cheese shavings to the top and baked the macaroni for five minutes so it would melt, and Riquet really enjoyed it that way.

Salina picked up beef, mushrooms and noodles and prepared a beef noodle dish for dinner. Quick, easy and tasty. She prepared a plate for Jake and kept it in the microwave, but when seven-twenty rolled around and he hadn't shown up yet, Salina put the dinner in the fridge.

She went back to Riquet, who was coloring in the living room, and sat beside her, watching her work on her latest masterpieces.

She'd had a good first day with the little girl. They had shared a lot of laughs as Ed had driven them from one activity to the other, Riquet regaling Salina with stories about some of the kids in her preschool. For such a young girl, she was quite perceptive.

Riquet had a bubbly and vivacious personality. She truly was a darling, and a joy to work with.

Having worked with some kids who had been spoiled and selfish, this was a welcome change. While Salina loved children in general, she hadn't liked the way some at the day care where she'd worked had had an appetite for all the latest gadgets at such a young age. Hand-held gaming devices were her biggest pet peeve. Riquet seemed to relish the joy of being a normal little girl. That meant that she enjoyed coloring, drawing, singing, watching television and using her hands and her imagination to entertain herself.

There was no Wii in the apartment, no Xbox 360 and the girl didn't even have a Nintendo DS. Salina was relieved. She saw some parents introduce these electronic gaming devices into their children's lives at too young an age, and she felt it was totally inappropriate. Clearly, Jake was a conscientious father, and Salina admired that about him.

At seven-thirty, Salina said, "Time for your bath, Riquet." The girl was to have her bath, and by eight o'clock be dressed and ready for bed.

"Does your father come home late every night?" Salina couldn't help asking Riquet as she bathed her a short while later.

Riquet nodded. "Mmm-hmm. He works all the time," she added sadly.

Twenty minutes later, Salina had Riquet out of the bath,

dressed in her pajamas and lying in her canopy bed that was filled with stuffed animals. She read the story Riquet requested, after which she gave her a kiss on the forehead and turned out the lights.

Still no Jake.

Emma hadn't been kidding when she said the man was a workaholic. Salina could totally see now why he preferred a nanny to be of the live-in variety. If he got home too late, all Salina would be able to do was head to her sister's apartment, climb into bed and get up the next morning to start the day over again.

She was glad she'd brought her suitcase with her.

Waiting until nine o'clock was all she could handle, because it had been a tiring day. Salina left a note for Jake, letting him know that his dinner was in the fridge and simply needed to be warmed up.

And then she retired to her own bedroom, got undressed and went to the bathroom to take a shower.

She was back in the bedroom, naked as the day she was born, when the door suddenly opened.

Chapter 5

Salina had no time to react. She should have said something—screamed or called out—but by the time the thought came to her, it was too late. Jake was standing in the bedroom.

Staring at her totally naked body.

She saw his eyes widen and his expression morph from surprised into mortification. That's when she sprang into action, grabbing the towel she had tossed onto the bed, in a futile attempt to cover her body. What was the point now? He had already seen her in the buff.

"Oh, God!" Jake exclaimed, quickly backing up. "I'm so sorry. I knocked—you didn't answer—God, I feel like an idiot."

Salina said nothing, just scrambled backward into the bathroom. There she sank onto the bathtub's edge and let out an angst-filled breath. Oh, Dear Lord, the man had just seen her without her clothes on!

Salina sat in the bathroom, not moving for a good five minutes. She was embarrassed. Never had a man she hadn't intended to, seen her without any clothes on.

And the last person she wanted to see her like this was her employer.

It's okay, it's okay, she repeated to herself. *It's not the end of the world. It was an accident, no big deal. Jake's probably seen plenty of women naked in his lifetime.*

But despite the words she told herself, Salina still felt awkward. How could she face him again, after such a humiliating moment?

She allowed herself a few more minutes of wallowing in embarrassment before she got up, got dressed in her pajamas, slipped a robe on top of that and then went out to see Jake.

He was sitting on the sofa, his head hanging low. When he saw her, he looked up and said, "Salina, I couldn't be more sorry. I knocked, and when you didn't answer, I thought maybe you were lying down. I just wanted to check on you, see how your day went. I am the world's biggest idiot, and I hope you don't think poorly of me. I behaved inappropriately, infringing on your privacy. I'm truly, truly sorry for that."

Hearing Jake apologize so profusely, Salina realized that she wasn't the only one who was humiliated. In fact, judging by his expression, he might feel even worse than she did.

She offered him a small smile and joined him on the sofa. "Don't beat yourself up," she began. "It was an accident. I'm not the first naked woman you've seen," she added good-naturedly, hoping to put his mind at ease, when in fact, humiliation was still flowing through her veins. It was a weird thing to have someone see you naked when you weren't planning on it.

Jake groaned, the sound telling her that he would probably feel guilty about this for a long while. He didn't meet her eyes.

"Hey," Salina said softly. "Look at me."

Slowly, Jake met her gaze. Salina held his eyes, silently letting him know that it was okay. It had been embarrassing, yes, but certainly she would survive. And someday she would be able to laugh about the moment.

And as she stared into Jake's eyes, something happened. She felt a frisson of heat. She had felt it before—indeed, she had felt a spark of attraction for Jake the very first time she had met him. And seeing him yesterday, too, she had been reminded of just how gorgeous he was. Something about him spoke to her on a level she didn't understand, but she had been prepared to ignore the feelings.

But now...

Now, she suddenly felt different. Because, looking into Jake's eyes, she felt heat warming her body from her center, and rolling out to every other part of her. There was something smoldering in Jake's eyes, something beyond the guilt that he had been feeling moments ago.

Jake was the one to look away. He stood abruptly and walked toward the dining room. "I see you left me some dinner. Thank you. But I'm sorry you went to the trouble. You didn't need to."

"Did you already eat?"

"Yes," Jake admitted. "I ordered in at the office. I should've told you. It wasn't on the schedule that you needed to prepare something for me, so..." His voice trailed off.

So he lived and died by his schedule, did he?

"Maria already knows that about me. But of course, she's worked for me for two years. I should have been more explicit in my instructions to you."

"It's okay," Salina said. "I just figured—I was making dinner anyway, why not make some for you? I'm happy to do that for you, if you like. As I told you earlier today, I really love cooking. If you call and tell me the time you'll be getting home, then I can better judge—"

"You don't need to go to all that trouble," Jake told her.

"It's no trouble."

"All the same, I don't want to bother you."

He was back to not looking at her. Clearly, he still felt bad about what had happened.

Or was it something else?

"I suppose you've had a long day and simply want to unwind," Salina said quickly. "I'll get out of your hair."

Feeling slightly discomfited, she spun around and hustled back to her bedroom.

Only when Jake was certain that Salina was out of sight did he sink into the plush leather chair at his dining room table. He buried his face in his hands.

He felt like a complete idiot. How could he have just opened the door and entered her room when he hadn't heard a response from her? He should have figured that maybe she'd been showering. It was just that Maria had always showered in the morning.

Maria, Maria… Oh, man. It was becoming more evident with each passing moment that Salina was *not* Maria.

The sight of her naked… Dear God. In that first moment as he'd seen her, before common sense had kicked in and told him that what was happening was wrong, he had seen a vision more lovely than he could have ever imagined.

Salina was beautiful on the outside, on the inside, and she was sexy as hell without any clothes on.

Jake pounded his forehead with his closed fist. Did he have a right to even think that? He had seen her by accident. He had unwittingly violated her privacy, and here he was enjoying the memory of her naked body. Surely that was wrong.

But, Lord, she was a vision of loveliness. Jake may have buried himself in work after Janine's death, telling himself that he would never love another woman, but he was still a man and couldn't help reacting to one.

That was all too clear right now. His entire body was thrumming with sexual awareness. It was a reaction that surprised him.

He found it hard to look at her already, having felt a definite reaction to her beauty, as it was. Now that he knew what she looked like naked—how would he ever face her again?

He could only hope that Maria returned from Mexico sooner, rather than later, and that his life as he had known it would return to normal.

Jake was avoiding her.

That was completely clear to Salina. Ever since he had seen her naked, he had barely looked at her. Two more days had passed, and he had busied himself getting ready in the mornings, telling her not to worry about making breakfast for him. He came home late in the evening and went to his bedroom almost immediately. He wasn't unpleasant. But it was clear that he was doing his best to not have to spend any meaningful time with her.

They were acting as if they had once been lovers, for goodness sake—former lovers who now had to share the same space and felt awkward with each other.

Yes, Salina got that he felt bad—but shouldn't she be the one who felt worse? She'd been the one caught in the buff. She had gotten over it. Why hadn't Jake?

She even suspected that he had told her she could go home on Friday night, that he would be staying at home on Saturday, simply because he didn't want to have her around.

Salina found herself wondering if she had totally misjudged Jake. Not misjudged his honor, that wasn't in doubt. But for a moment, as she had stared into his eyes after the incident, she thought she felt something spark between them.

A spark of mutual attraction.

Now, with the way he was avoiding her, she wondered if she had misread him completely. If she, clearly drawn to his good looks and decent nature, had been reading into things with him because she wanted something to be there that wasn't.

She returned to Jake's condo on Sunday evening, shortly after six. She had the concierge call up to the apartment to announce her arrival, and when she got to his door, she knocked instead of using the key. Jake opened the door, but it was Riquet who scurried past him and threw her arms around Salina's legs. At least one of them was happy to see her.

"I've missed you!" the little girl exclaimed.

"I missed you, too," Salina said, smiling. It felt good to be back. She hugged Riquet long and hard, and then released her and looked at Jake. "Hi, Jake."

Jake smiled stiffly. "Hi."

Salina wanted to roll her eyes. She wanted to tell him, *Enough already. You saw me naked. Let's move on.* But she did no such thing.

"We just started watching a movie," Riquet announced.

"Oh, yeah? Which one?"

"The Tale of Despereaux," Jake answered. "You missed about fifteen minutes. Feel free to join us if you want. But it's an animated movie, so don't feel obligated to watch it if you don't want to."

"Are you kidding? I love animated movies."

"It's about a mouse," Riquet explained, tugging on Salina's hand and pulling her into the living room. "It lives in the castle."

"Ahh," Salina said. "I remember seeing the commercials about it. Have you seen *Ratatouille?* The one about the rat who wants to be a chef?" When Riquet shook her head, Salina continued. "That's an excellent movie. We'll have to watch that one sometime."

Riquet plopped down onto the sofa and Salina sat beside her on the right. Jake sat on the other side of Riquet.

Salina soon realized that, while Riquet had said *we,* she should have said *I.* Jake wasn't really paying attention to the movie. He sat with a folder on his lap, and he was going through a file, making notes. A laptop was open and on the coffee table in front of him.

A Sunday night, and still he wasn't taking a break from work.

Before the movie was even over he got up, gathered the file and his laptop and went to the bedroom.

Salina rolled over in bed when she heard the soft rapping on her door. She knew it was late, and a quick glance at the clock told her it was 1:23 a.m.

"Are you awake?" she heard Jake ask from the other side of the door.

Salina sat up. "Yes."

Jake entered the room. Salina's breath caught in her throat when she saw that he only wore a white towel wrapped around his waist.

"What are you doing?" Salina asked.

Jake stepped forward, his movements slow and deliberate, his gaze holding hers.

Salina swallowed.

Jake loosened the towel and let it fall to the floor. Salina's jaw dropped.

"I saw you naked," he began. "I think it's only fair that I return the favor."

Salina gaped at Jake, taking in his nude form in all its glory. She began to feel hot, her chest becoming tight.

And then her eyes popped open.

Instantly, they flitted back and forth around the dark room. At first she was disoriented. But as she looked around, realized that she was lying in the bed, that the room was dark and quiet, and—more importantly—that she was alone, she knew that she had been dreaming.

Good Lord, what a dream! Her skin was actually flushed from the very idea that Jake had entered her room and gotten naked. And while it had only been a dream, she found that her breathing was ragged.

She was *dreaming* about Jake McKnight.

What on earth was happening to her?

She closed her eyes and tried to shake the man from her thoughts. Instead, she kept imagining what he might look like naked.

It's only fair that I return the favor... That should have clued her in to the fact that she was dreaming. What a ridiculous line.

The entire dream was ridiculous.

And yet Salina's body felt flushed because of it.

She rolled over onto her stomach and closed her eyes. But she couldn't banish from her mind the image of a nude Jake.

And she couldn't help wondering if he would look as good naked in real life as he did in her dream.

Chapter 6

"I want to bake a cake for daddy." Riquet announced a few days later. She took the last bite of her peanut butter and jelly sandwich, the snack she had requested instead of macaroni and cheese. She was home for her lunch after preschool and was due to meet with Sarah for her play date within the hour.

"You do?" Salina asked. She added more milk to Riquet's cup.

"Uh-huh. I want to bake it for today, when he comes home from work."

"We can't do it for tonight, honey," Salina said. "You've got your play date, and then ballet—"

"I don't want to go."

"You're supposed to meet with Sarah, remember?"

"I don't want to go," Riquet reiterated. "I want to stay home today. And bake a cake."

Salina couldn't blame the girl. With her numerous activities, she couldn't help thinking that for someone so young,

Riquet was overscheduled. There were times Salina wanted to discuss just that with Jake, but she knew it wasn't her place to do so.

"Please," Riquet begged. "Please can I stay home today and bake a cake with you for daddy?"

Forget Riquet's schedule. Salina would call Sarah's mother and tell her that she and Riquet couldn't make it today.

"Oh, all right," Salina conceded. "What kind of cake do you want to make? A cheesecake, or maybe something—"

"A birthday cake," Riquet said, cutting Salina off. "Because when it was his birthday, he didn't have a party. He didn't even have a cake!"

"He didn't?" Salina asked, taking a seat beside Riquet.

The young girl shook her head robustly. "He said he was too busy, and he would have a cake next year."

"Next year? Well, that's not good."

"You should always have a cake," Riquet said, with all the wisdom of a four-year-old. "Your birthday only comes once a year, so it's special."

"When was his birthday?"

Riquet pursed her lips in thought. "A week ago, I think. Or maybe last month. Something like that."

Jake had had a birthday without any noticeable celebration at all? Not even for his daughter's sake? Salina could only imagine that, for a man who was married to his work, a birthday was an unnecessary distraction.

But Riquet was right. Birthdays were important. Especially as a way to create happy memories with your child.

"You know what," Salina began, "I think that's a great idea. We'll make a cake for your dad as a surprise. I know he's going to love it. It will be a belated birthday party, so he won't even expect it."

"What's 'belated'?"

"That means when you do something after the day you

should have. Like if your birthday was two weeks ago, but
you can't have a party until later than the date of your birthday. That's belated."

"Oh. So we're going to have a belated party for daddy."

Salina was already picturing it. It would start with dinner,
a family dinner—not Jake eating on his own as he went over
legal briefs. And then dessert. A cake that she and Riquet
would make together.

"Your father is going to love this surprise," Salina said.
She would make certain of it. "What kind of cake do you
want to make for him?"

"Chocolate!" Riquet exclaimed with excitement.

"Chocolate it is." Rising, Salina walked the short distance
to the cupboards and pantry and searched for any kind of
cake mix, but found nothing. There was flour, but not a lot.
Which was for the best, she decided. Because she would
make Jake a special cake from scratch.

Which meant she would have to take a trip to the store.
It would be a little adventure for her and Riquet. She had a
wonderful recipe from scratch for chocolate cake that would
be much better than the ready-made mixes that came in a
convenient box. It would take a bit of time to prepare, but
she and Riquet had time. If Jake kept up with his typical
routine, he wouldn't be back before 7:00 p.m.

"Let's get you washed up," Salina said to Riquet. "Because we have to go to the store to buy everything we need
to make the best cake ever!"

Before they left for the store, Salina called Sarah's mother
and told her that she and Riquet weren't going to be able to
make the play date. Then she called Jake at the office. His
phone went to voice mail, so she left him a message, letting
him know not to eat on the run before he got home. She also
requested that he try to leave work early, so he could be home
for dinner at six-thirty. "Riquet said she'd really like to have

dinner with you tonight, so I hope you can make this work," Salina added, before she hung up.

Jake spent so much time at work, pouring every ounce of his energy into some big lawsuit he was working on, and generally not enjoying much of a home life. She had never seen him sit down and enjoy a meal without having his case files beside him. And he came home so late that he ate by himself, not with his daughter.

Salina would give him the gift of a home-cooked meal and time with his daughter—an evening to commemorate the birthday he hadn't bothered to acknowledge.

And maybe she and Jake would finally have some time to sit down and chat and get to know each other a little better.

A short while later, Salina was at the store with Riquet. In addition to buying the ingredients she needed to make the chocolate cake, she also bought a fresh chicken. Since she was going to be making a cake that would require more time in the kitchen, she needed the meal to be something that would be easier to prepare. Her roast chicken was scrumptious, if she did say so herself. It never failed to leave her friends' and family's mouths watering.

She hoped that Jake would enjoy it, and that he would appreciate the time to sit down as a family and enjoy a meal.

Not that she was family…but she didn't like the fact that they were pretty much like two ships passing in the night. A part of her heart ached for him, seeing how much time he spent working and not enjoying his life. She wondered if he had always been this way, or if he'd only become like this in the wake of his wife's death.

She hated the idea that Jake was perhaps hiding from life—hiding because he couldn't deal with his pain. He had a little girl who was overscheduled, one he should be spending more time with. Hadn't life itself taught him that time was guaranteed to no one?

Salina wasn't naive. Ever since that dream about Jake coming into her room naked, she couldn't deny to herself that her feelings were growing for him. It wasn't what she had expected, but her attraction for him was real. It was an attraction she'd felt the very first time she met him—inexplicable but undeniable, and she sensed it wasn't one-sided. If only he would stop avoiding her, maybe they could actually see if there was any potential between them.

Salina put the thought out of her mind and concentrated on making a meal that Jake could enjoy without any distractions.

Back at the apartment, Riquet was excited to get started with the cooking, and it did Salina's heart good to see her so happy about helping to prepare the special meal for the evening. She helped Salina put the various seasonings on the bird, and was quite proud of her involvement in the dinner-making process. Once the chicken was in the oven, she and Salina set about making the cake.

Riquet went at the cake-making challenge with gusto. Much of the flour ended up on the counter and on the kitchen floor, but that was okay. If she wanted to help, Salina had no problem with that. In fact, she didn't like when parents and teachers didn't allow children to be involved in various activities because they didn't want them to make a mess. As far as she was concerned, doing an activity together like this created bonding time. The mess could be cleaned up. The experience would be priceless for the child.

Because of the fact that Jake had dual ovens, it allowed Salina to put the cake into one of them to bake while the chicken was also cooking. It was perfect.

Boy, she could get used to this kitchen…

Riquet helped set the table, even adding a floral vase from a nearby window ledge for décor. And as the cake was cooling, Salina and Riquet also worked on making fresh icing. The secret to Salina's smooth, rich icing was butter and honey with a hint of lemon juice. People always loved it.

"I want to put the icing on the cake!" Riquet said, once the mixture was complete.

Salina showed Riquet how to gently put the icing on the cake using a spatula. She applied some, then Riquet applied some, and while the cake was not aesthetically a masterpiece when it was finished, it was made with love, and therefore was one of the best cakes Salina had ever seen. She hoped that Jake would like it.

When, finally, the door sounded, Salina's stomach knotted. She took Riquet's hand and hurried with her to the foyer as they had planned. When the door opened they both began to sing. "Happy birthday to you, happy birthday to you, happy birthday dear Daddy, happy birthday to you!"

And Salina wasn't sure why, but she felt her throat fill with emotion. It was the look on Riquet's face, how happy she was with her big surprise. Salina realized that she really was becoming attached to the little girl.

And not just to the girl. But to the dad.

Because there was something about Jake that made Salina want to be the one to make him whole again. She didn't understand it. The feeling had been sudden—it started the first night she met him and witnessed the sadness in his eyes. But it was real, a feeling she knew she couldn't deny.

Jake looked at both Salina and Riquet with narrowed eyes. "It's not my birthday," he said.

"Maybe not today," Salina began, "but Riquet tells me that it was your birthday a couple of weeks back?"

"Three weeks, actually," Jake explained.

"And you didn't even have a cake," Salina said, placing both hands on her hips in mild reproof.

"You're always supposed to have a party, Daddy," Riquet said. "But you're always so busy working."

Jake lowered himself onto his haunches and placed his hands on Riquet's arms. "I'm sorry," he said. "You're right. I have been working a lot. I should've had a party for my birthday."

Riquet wrapped her arms around her father's neck and hugged him, and seeing this moment of closeness made Salina get a little choked up. It was nice to see this bonding between father and daughter.

"It was Riquet's idea to surprise you," Salina explained as Jake stood.

"Something definitely smells good," Jake said.

"Why don't you offload your things, get washed up and come to the dining room when you're ready," Salina told him.

Jake headed to the bedroom and Salina went to the kitchen. She got the tossed salad from the fridge, put the steamed carrots into a ceramic bowl and brought both items to the table. Then she took the chicken out of the oven, put it on a serving plate and set it on the table, as well. The table was already set with drinking glasses, dishes and cutlery, and all that was needed now was the dinner. She put the carving knife with the bird so that Jake could do the honors of the cutting, the way her father always had done in their home.

When he came into the dining room and glanced at the table, he looked even more surprised. "You made a turkey?"

"No, not a turkey," Salina explained. "It's a roast chicken. Fresh out of the oven. I kept it warming until you got here. Thank you for coming at six-thirty, by the way. It was really important to Riquet. And to me," she added softly. "You work all the time, and Riquet really misses you. I know you're busy, and you've got an important job to do. But Riquet's too young to really understand that. All she really wants is to spend more time with you. And there's something a little sad about you coming home so late and eating by yourself, when the meal isn't fresh anymore...." Salina paused, realizing she was rambling. "I thought it was time you enjoyed a sit-down family dinner."

"Thank you for going to the trouble."

But despite the words he said, there was an expression on his face that seemed disturbed.

No, *pained.*

It was a look that made Salina's heart drop.

Jake fixated on the three table settings, a feeling of unease gripping his heart. He was suddenly thinking about the last time he sat down just like this with his daughter and his late wife. At the time, there had been no reason to believe that they had anything other than a bright future to look forward to. There was no warning that the next day, when his wife left the house to go visit her parents in upstate New York, she would be involved in a tragic car accident and never return home.

"You don't like it," Salina said softly, clearly picking up on his mood.

He shook his head. "No, of course I do."

"Then what's wrong?"

How could he tell her? How could he tell her that her gesture had reminded him of family and all that he had lost? If he was honest with himself, he had to admit that ever since Salina started to work for him, he had been thinking about family all the more. For a full six months he had mourned his wife, and in the year and a half that followed, he had tried to block the memories of her and their life together from his mind. He'd had to do that for his sanity.

But now Salina was a part of his life, and he found himself missing the companionship of a woman. And not just friendship. But companionship in the way that he had experienced it with Janine.

Something about Salina made him long for a family life again. Maybe it was the way that she so easily related to Riquet, and even something like this—where she must've spent a good amount of time cooking with his daughter and overall being like a mom to her—but it touched him on a level he thought had been closed off forever.

Salina was only supposed to be involved in their lives for a few weeks at most, and yet she seemed indelibly imprinted on the fabric of their home life now.

"It's perfect," Jake told her, meaning it. "Thank you."

Salina smiled. It was a smile that was completely endearing and charming. Jake found himself thinking not for the first time just how beautiful she was.

He didn't plan it when he reached for her hand and squeezed it. He saw the look of surprise in her face, surprise he himself felt. He quickly released her hand and cleared his throat.

"We even made you a cake, Daddy," Riquet said.

"You did?"

"All afternoon. It was hard work!"

Riquet's words suddenly registered. "All afternoon? You mean—"

"She really wanted to do this for you," Salina began. "She asked if she could stay home this afternoon, miss her play date and ballet. I hope you don't mind. If you saw the way she asked me, it clearly meant so much to her, I couldn't say no."

Salina was offering him an explanation as though she thought he would be unhappy. Jake waved off her apology.

"It's fine," he told her. "Sometimes we all need a break. Even four-year-olds."

"Come see the cake," Riquet said to him. She looked so happy as she reached for his hand, it drove home the point to Jake that he was spending entirely too much time at the office. Yes, he had a job to do that required a lot of hours, but he should equally be putting time into being a father.

Riquet led him into the kitchen, where the cake rested on one corner of the counter.

Jake's mouth fell open. When Salina had said that they'd baked a cake, he hadn't expected this.

This cake before him wasn't your regular home-baked sort. This one was tall and elaborately decorated with chocolate icing and Smarties. It reminded him of the kind of cake you saw in windows when you passed specialty shops.

On top was written "Happy Birthday Daddy!" It was just a birthday cake, but judging by the ear-to-ear smile on Riquet's face, it meant the world to her.

Jake swallowed the emotion lodging in his throat.

"Do you like it, Daddy?" Riquet asked.

"Like it? I love it. This looks like the best chocolate cake ever."

He dipped his finger into the icing and then brought it to his mouth. Once he had tasted it, his sentiment was confirmed. It had to be the most delectable chocolate icing he had ever tried. He could only imagine that the cake would be equally as delicious.

"Why do I get the feeling this isn't Betty Crocker?" he asked.

"Because I made it from scratch," Salina said, smiling brightly. "Actually, we both did."

Jake stared at her. Really stared at her, his eyes meeting with and holding hers. He didn't avert his gaze as he had been doing for days. He stared at her and saw in her eyes that spark he had the first time he met her.

And like the first time, it filled him with warmth.

And it made him think about something he had long since given up on.

The possibility of finding love.

Again.

Chapter 7

The loud cry jarred Salina awake. For the first moment, she was confused. Then she thought, *Riquet.*

Immediately she jumped out of bed. She raced out of her bedroom to Riquet's room. She flung the door open and ran inside, where she found the girl sitting up in her bed, crying uncontrollably.

"Oh, sweetheart," Salina said as she rushed toward her. She sank onto the bed beside Riquet and wrapped her arms around her. "What's wrong, honey?"

The sound of feet pounding the floor drew Salina's attention to the door. Jake suddenly appeared, a look of concern marring his handsome features. He hurried into the room.

"Riquet," he began, lowering himself onto the bed beside Salina. He reached for Riquet, taking her from Salina's arms and gathering her into his. "Sweetheart, what's the matter?"

"I had a bad dream," the girl explained. "I was so scared."

"It's okay now," he told her. "You're fine. Daddy's here."

Salina watched as Riquet rested her head against Jake's

chest. He cradled her head gently and cooed her. As Riquet calmed down, Jake looked at Salina, as if registering her for the first time, his eyes sweeping over her and taking in her short nightgown.

He quickly glanced away, and Salina knew that he was remembering the time he had walked into the room when she'd been naked.

She, however, let her eyes linger on Jake's body. With all the commotion over Riquet's distress, she hadn't initially noticed his state of dress—or, rather, undress—as he had come running into the room. Now, she took it all in in one slow glance. He wore only boxer shorts. His naked chest and arms were immaculately sculpted.

Lord, but the man was gorgeous…

The moment that thought came to her, Salina felt bad for checking him out, and quickly jerked her gaze away.

She glanced at the Princess Tiana clock on the wall: 3:41 a.m. "Would you like some warm milk?" she asked Riquet. Maybe some warm milk would help her get back to sleep.

Riquet shook her head. "I'm okay. I just had a bad dream."

"We're okay for now," Jake told Salina. "Go on and head back to bed."

"Oh." Salina rose. "Sure."

"What was the dream?" she heard Jake ask Riquet as she made her way to the door.

"I was dreaming that you were in a car," Riquet explained. "And that you got into a really bad accident, and I was crying so hard…."

The words made Salina halt. What a horrible dream! The poor girl, fearing that she might lose her father the way she had lost her mother.

Salina glanced over her shoulder and saw Jake hugging Riquet tightly. "Oh, honey. Don't you worry. I'm not going anywhere, okay? I'm not leaving you."

Salina watched Jake gently cradling his daughter a moment longer, then, feeling like an intruder on this intimate moment, she quietly left the room.

At the sound of the soft rapping on her door, Salina sat up in her bed, alarmed. Was there a problem with Riquet for which Jake needed her? Perhaps he wanted her to make that warm milk, after all.

"Yes?" Salina called.

No response. A few seconds later there was more knocking on her door.

"Yes," she said, a little louder this time. "You can open the door."

The door opened, and Jake stepped into the room. And she couldn't help thinking of the fantasy she'd had the previous week, in which Jake entered her room wearing only a towel.

Today, he was wearing black boxer shorts. He had a robe, she knew, but he hadn't bothered to go back to his bedroom to put it on. Perhaps he didn't think it was a big deal, given that Salina had seen him only ten minutes before clad in those sexy boxers of his.

"I came by to say that I hope you weren't offended by me telling you to leave Riquet's room," he said.

"No." Salina shook her head. "No, of course not. Is she okay?"

"Yeah, she's fine."

"Good."

Jake paused. He seemed to be gathering his thoughts. "I also came by because I wanted to thank you."

Salina gave him a quizzical look.

"For rushing into the room so quickly," Jake explained.

"You don't need to thank me for that," Salina said. "I heard Riquet crying. How could I not go to her?"

"Still, I wanted to thank you. I'm not sure I've made it clear to you just how much I appreciate the job you're doing with my daughter."

Salina nodded, grateful for the compliment. "You're welcome."

Jake stepped farther into the room, and Salina's heart rate accelerated. Clearly, he wanted to say something else to her.

Or did he want to *do* something else? Perhaps kiss her?

"Do you mind if I sit for a moment?" he asked.

Her heart beat even faster. "No. Go ahead."

"I want to thank you for something else," he went on. "You said something at dinner, something that really hit home with me. You talked about how Riquet really misses me. I never thought about that. But I see now that you're right. I'm working all the time, and it must affect her. You were right to point out that she simply needs to have her dad around sometimes. That's the reason I asked you to leave us alone for the moment. I wanted to be the one to offer comfort for a change."

Salina hadn't considered that he may have been thinking that, but she understood his reasoning. "You don't have to explain that. You had every right to spend that private time with your daughter."

"All the same, I didn't want you to think that I didn't appreciate your efforts, because I do. In fact, you've been great. More than I could have hoped for in Maria's absence."

Pausing, Jake stared at her. Really stared. Salina stared back, her breath catching as heat spread across her belly.

Did he want to kiss her?

But just as quickly as the thought came to Salina, the moment between them passed. Looking away, Jake suddenly stood.

"Thank you, again," he said.

"Wait," Salina blurted out. She wasn't ready for this moment between them to be over.

Jake looked at her. "Yes?"

"Can I ask you something?"

He nodded. "Sure."

"I'm just wondering," Salina began, then halted. "I'm wondering if you always come home from work so late, or..." Her voice trailed off. Something had made her want to ask Jake this question, but she was suddenly unsure that she should.

"Or?" Jake prompted.

Maybe it was because he was here in her room and they were finally having a real conversation, but she decided to speak what was on her mind. "Or...have you been coming home late to avoid me?"

"Avoid you?"

"Ever since you walked in on me naked," Salina began sheepishly. Her throat was suddenly thick, and she swallowed. "I just got that impression...maybe I'm wrong."

"No," Jake said. "Not at all."

"You're sure?"

"Absolutely," he stressed.

"Good. I hate the idea that there's any awkwardness between us."

"Please put that thought out of your mind," Jake said. "Like I said, I'm very pleased with the job you're doing."

"Tell me about her," Salina said suddenly, surprising herself. "Tell me about your late wife."

Jake looked momentarily stunned, as though he hadn't expected her to ask that. In fact, Salina was sure that he hadn't. They'd never talked about her before.

Jake asked, "What do you want to know?"

"What was she like? I know she liked to ride horses. But that's all I know. Did she work outside the home? What was her passion?"

For a long moment Jake simply stood there, his face scrunched in thought. Salina almost expected that he might turn and leave the room.

Instead, he sat back down. "I haven't really talked about her much…since she died."

"You don't have to—"

"No," Jake said, interrupting her. "It's okay. One of the things I've suddenly realized is that I've done my best to avoid dealing with what happened. Sure, I know she's gone—I can't avoid that—but I've tried to block the pain. I think that's why I've been working so much, and it's taken you to make me realize that Riquet is probably suffering for that."

"Riquet is a very well-adjusted, pleasant and happy child. Please don't be offended by what I said about her needing to spend more time with you. You did that tonight, by coming home for a family dinner and surprise birthday party, and that sort of thing goes a long way. I'm sure Riquet will remember this evening for years to come."

"All the same, I know that I haven't been the kind of father I was when Janine was alive."

Jake blew out a weary breath. Salina stayed silent, waiting for him to speak.

"Janine was a stay-at-home mom. Her only goal was to have a house full of children, which I supported. I'm an only child myself, and I never wanted that for my daughter."

"I can see that. Riquet would do well with some brothers and sisters."

"I suppose you could say *I* was Janine's passion. As well as Riquet, of course. She supported me fully. Whatever my goals were, she wanted to help me realize them."

"Are you speaking about something specific?" Salina asked.

He nodded. "For a long time, I've considered entering the political arena."

"Really?"

"Yeah. My father was a mayor for several years in a town outside of Atlanta, then went on to run for the senate. He started off as a Baptist minister, actually."

"Really?" Salina asked, amazed.

"Yep. He and my mother have always expected me to continue the legacy—not as a minister, but in politics. Make a name for myself in law, move on to city politics, then beyond. Maybe even one day take a run for the White House."

"You're kidding."

"Nope. My father was in politics for many years. Ultimately, he went back to being a preacher. He was offered a position as the head of a church in Hoboken, and he and my mother moved from Georgia to New Jersey. In part because it gave them the opportunity to be closer to me and Riquet." Jake paused. "I met Janine because of my father's political connections. Her father was a city councilor in Albany. I was attending some political function with my parents, she was there with her father...and we hit it off."

"You loved her," Salina said softly.

"Yes. We were happy together. Our relationship wasn't perfect, but we were happy. And then it ended. In an instant, she was gone."

Jake stood suddenly. Salina knew that this was hard for him, and couldn't blame him for not wanting to continue talking about the woman he had lost.

"I didn't mean to bring you down," she said.

"You didn't." Jake shrugged. "It is what it is."

"If you ever want to talk, I'm here. I just want you to know that."

Jake nodded.

"Can I ask what this case is that you're working on?"

Salina said. She was making more conversation because she wasn't yet ready for him to leave. "You haven't told me anything about it, other than mention that it's a class action lawsuit."

As the words left her mouth, she realized that Jake was under no obligation to tell her anything about it. "I mean, you don't have to. I guess… I guess I just want you to know that anything you might want to talk about, I'm happy to lend an ear."

"I appreciate that."

Salina nodded and got the sense that he was going to leave the room. If so, she wasn't going to push the issue. She had taken up enough of his time, and they both needed to get up in the morning.

So she was surprised when Jake said, "It's a huge class-action lawsuit. It has to do with an asthma medication that affected many people in horrible ways. Some died. Some had other major complications. I won't bore you with all the details, but the settlement could be one of the biggest in US history. The number of complainants is growing every day."

"Wow."

"Sometimes these drug companies rush a product onto the market because they want to make a profit, without thinking about the effects on the real people who are going to be using the drug. That's what happened here. They rushed this miracle medication, even though some researchers believed there could be potential problems. The company has to pay for this kind of negligence. They have to understand that people's lives are irreparably damaged when they put profit over product."

Now it made sense why Jake was working so hard. He was working on a major class-action lawsuit, perhaps one of the biggest in history.

"Are all the partners working on the case?" Salina asked.

She knew there were four partners at the firm. Her sister hoped to one day become one.

"Yes. It's taking a lot of man-hours. The case will be on-going for at least the next couple of years."

"You're obviously very dedicated to your job."

"If you're not passionate about something, then you shouldn't do it—and I've always been passionate about the law. For me, this is how I can make a difference."

"You really are an incredible man," Salina said, surprised to hear that the words had come out low and throaty.

Jake's eyes widened slightly. And then they grew darker. Salina recognized the change for what it was, and her breath caught in her throat.

Desire. She saw desire in Jake's eyes.

Suddenly, he was reaching for her hand. Lifting it to his mouth. Kissing her palm. Then the inside of her wrist...and oh, that sent a charge of heat straight up her arm.

He inched forward, slipping his hand around her waist as he did. And before Salina could even register that this was really happening, Jake brought his mouth down onto hers.

And, God! The sensation that flooded her body. Warm and tingly and intoxicating.

His mouth played over hers tenderly for several seconds, their lips softly connecting in the sweetest of kisses. Then Jake flicked the tip of his tongue over her bottom lip before gently nipping on it, and Salina opened her mouth wider, wanting more of him.

His tongue swept into her mouth, teasing hers with deliciously slow strokes. Sighing with pleasure, Salina slipped her hands around his neck and savored this amazing moment.

But suddenly, Jake was tearing his lips from hers and jerking backward. Salina had been on an emotional high, but now she came crashing back to earth.

Jake quickly stood. "I'm sorry," he said, and he didn't look at her.

"Jake—"

But he rushed to the door without even turning back.

And then he was gone.

What the hell had he just done?

That was the thought coming into Jake's mind, over and over again, as he lay on his king-size bed.

He was hard. *Hard,* for goodness sake. Hot and hard and wishing that he hadn't left Salina's room. Wishing that he had instead gone from A to Z—taken her clothes off and made sweet love to her.

"Damn it, Jake—what's happened to you?" he asked himself. This wasn't like him. He could see a pretty face and be unaffected. And yet here he was, craving sex with his child's nanny.

Salina was more than a nanny. She was an incredible woman. He could tell that, even though he hadn't known her for that long.

More and more, he found her irresistible. It didn't matter that he had tried his best to limit their contact. Some people you simply clicked with, and for him, Salina was one of those people.

And it was more than the fact that he simply clicked with her—he felt a spark of life every time he was around her. What he felt was raw attraction, pure and simple.

He should have gotten up from the bed earlier. He had felt his desire for her growing every time he laid eyes on her, his resistance weakening, and he should have known that going into her bedroom was asking for trouble.

Or was that exactly *why* he had gone into her room—to see what would happen between them?

All he knew for sure was that, as he'd sat on the bed talking to her, he'd felt the strongest urge to pull her into his arms and kiss that sweet, full mouth of hers that had been tempting him since the first time he had laid eyes on her.

Then she'd given him that look, spoken in the soft and flirty voice, and he hadn't been able to control himself.

And God help him, the kiss had been more than he had expected it to be.

He was still aroused thinking about it, and damn near tempted to head back to her bedroom and finish what they'd started.

But he would do no such thing. He wasn't a man who gave in to his emotions. He controlled them—not the other way around.

As he lay in the dark staring at the ceiling, he asked himself, *What is it about her?*

Perhaps it was the way she interacted with his daughter. It was so natural, organic. Her manner was as experienced as if she had raised many children, and yet she wasn't a mother.

She didn't have that special touch with Riquet simply because she had worked in day care. That touch came from her heart.

That was getting to him, clearly. How great she was with Riquet, the joy and spontaneity she brought into his daughter's life.

She was good for Riquet.

And just maybe she was good for him, too.

Chapter 8

Salina could think of nothing but the kiss all the next day.

She had awoken with a sense of anticipation, looking forward to seeing Jake. For breakfast she'd even made the homemade pancakes for him that he loved so much. She had wanted to convey to him that she didn't have any regrets about the kiss, and put to rest the thought he might have that he'd taken advantage of her.

But Jake had stayed in his room later than usual in the morning, and when he made an appearance, he barely had time to utter a greeting, kiss Riquet goodbye and head out the door.

Salina's anticipation had deflated like a balloon that had been pricked with a pin. Was he so upset that he'd kissed her that he was back to avoiding her?

Well, Salina wouldn't have it. Not after a kiss that had literally rocked her world.

She went about her daily business as usual, taking Riquet

to preschool, doing some shopping for groceries, and was now back at Jake's apartment trying to decide what she should cook tonight. She wanted to create another meal Jake would love. But if his actions this morning were any indication, he was likely going to return home late, just so he wouldn't have to deal with her and what had happened the night before. If she was smart, she would cook a meal for Riquet and herself and forget about planning a meal for Jake that would likely go to waste.

But the truth was, she wanted another dinner like the last one. Time when they could all sit, share a meal and enjoy each other's company. She wanted many, many more of them.

She had picked up portabello mushrooms and chicken breasts because she was planning on making a chicken marsala meal. Now she was rethinking the decision. They'd had chicken last night, so perhaps she should have considered something else. Like veal. Really show Jake her culinary skills.

The way to a man's heart was his stomach, after all....

Too late now.

She went to the extensive wine rack in Jake's dining room and began to peruse it, looking for a red wine she could use to make the sauce for the chicken marsala. She was lifting a bottle when her cell phone rang. Putting the bottle back on the rack, she quickly ran to retrieve her phone from her purse, hoping it hadn't disturbed Riquet, who was napping on the sofa after a tiring day that involved a play date, gymnastics *and* a piano lesson. As she held up the phone, she saw her best friend Brianne's number flashing on the screen.

Salina immediately pressed the talk button and put the phone to her ear. "Hey, Brianne!" She walked back into the dining room and took a seat at the table. "What's up?"

It had been a while since Salina had been able to speak to her best friend in depth. The past few times they'd chatted had been when she was working for Donald, and she'd been too busy to have the kind of conversation she would have liked. Donald had been so harsh at the restaurant in those early days, that he would have given her an earful if he'd seen her sneaking in a few minutes on the phone in the back corner of the restaurant's kitchen.

And after the abysmal turn of events with the womanizing jerk, Salina had felt somewhat embarrassed to talk to Brianne and tell her what had transpired. So she hadn't bothered to call her.

"I'm great," Brianne said, and she sounded happier than Salina had known her to sound in years. Certainly not since her fiancé had disappeared in the Canadian Rockies three years ago that past November. Carter had been presumed dead, and Brianne had found it hard to move on, being the one person it seemed who believed that he might be alive somewhere and in need of help. She hadn't wanted to give up on the man she loved.

But Brianne's world had gone into a tailspin when Carter's former best friend, Alex, who had been with him on that fateful trip, showed up at her door a couple of months ago and told her that he thought Carter was actually alive. Brianne had gone with Alex to Florida to search for him, and Salina had been stunned to learn the update—that Carter had faked his death, and Brianne had fallen for Alex. Though Salina hadn't been *that* surprised that Brianne and Alex had found each other, because when she had met Alex, she thought he'd be perfect for Brianne.

"So everything's going great with Alex, I take it?" Salina asked.

"Couldn't be better, Salina." Brianne sighed happily. "I guess sometimes it takes a tragedy, throwing your world upside down, to help you find the person you're supposed to be with."

Brianne's words resonated with Salina. She wondered if Jake would ever come to feel that way. Then again, his tragedy had cost him the woman he had loved. A woman who had loved him—not deceived him the way Carter had deceived Brianne.

"I'm not surprised," Salina said. "I always knew Alex was the right guy for you."

"Really?" Brianne sounded shocked.

"Yep."

"Then why didn't you say so?"

"You were engaged to Carter, head over heels for him. It wasn't my place to say that I thought Alex would be a better match."

"But I don't get it," Brianne said. "I don't understand what made you think that."

"I can't explain it," Salina said. "All I can tell you is that when I saw you and Alex together, something just seemed right about that. There was something about his temperament that made me think he'd be ideal for you. Plus, I hated the way Carter was always having you obsess over your weight. I just got the sense that Alex liked you for you. I saw the way he looked at you, and it was with appreciation, not critical eyes."

"Wow. You just totally summed up the way it was. And I guess on some level I always knew that about Alex, too—but I'd gotten involved with Carter first…. And as they say, the rest is history." Brianne paused briefly. "Now for the best news. Alex and I are planning a late spring wedding!" she squealed. "Early June."

Salina squealed, too. "You're getting married! Oh, my God!"

"And you know you have to be in my wedding, so whatever you do, clear the date for June fourth."

"Absolutely! Ohhh, I'm going to make you the most fabulous wedding cake *ever.*"

"No, no, no. I don't want you to worry about making the cake. With you being in the wedding, you won't have time."

"I'm going to be in the wedding *and* I'm going to make your cake. Don't you worry about it."

Brianne giggled. "Okay. If you insist."

"It's not every day your best friend gets married. You'd better believe I insist."

"I can't argue with that," Brianne said. Then, "Enough about me. All we ever do is talk about me. I get the feeling you don't want to tell me what's happening in New York. Is everything okay?"

"As a matter of fact…" Salina took a few minutes to fill her friend in on all that had happened with Donald Martin and how she was now working temporarily as a nanny. "Crazy, I know, but that's where I am," she summed up. "I'm going to go to culinary school, become a chef the old-fashioned, hard way. No more shortcuts for me."

"I can't believe that jerk," Brianne said. "And I can't believe you're a nanny."

"Like I said, one of the partners at my sister's law firm needed someone immediately. Since I've had experience in day care, it just worked out."

"He's a widower, huh?"

"Yeah. It's a sad story. His wife died two years ago in a car accident."

"Oh, that's awful."

"I don't know how someone moves on after something like that," Salina commented. "I guess he's coped by throwing himself into work. I suppose that's easy to do when you're a lawyer. He's working on this major class-action lawsuit—he was telling me about it last night—and it's obvious he really cares about the cause. He's not just in it for the big settlement." Salina paused, a smile touching her lips as she re-membered being in the room with Jake the night before. As she remembered their kiss. "He's really smart, really nice, and all-round an incredible guy."

"Salina?" Brianne said, her tone probing.

"Yes?"

"You just told me quite a bit about Jake. Why do I feel there's something else—something more important—that you're leaving out?"

"Like what?"

"Oh, let me see. Is he cute?"

"Very," Salina answered with exuberance, then realized that Brianne would pick up on the tone.

"And he's single, right?"

"I already told you that."

"No, you said he's a widower. That doesn't mean he doesn't have a girlfriend. Is he dating?"

"No. As far as I know, he hasn't dated since his wife died."

"Aha!"

"Aha what?"

"It's totally obvious that you're attracted to him," Brianne summed up.

There was no point in denying the truth. And Salina wanted to tell someone. "I think he's amazing. He's gorgeous, a devoted father, and even though I never expected to blur the lines of professionalism with him, we kissed last night."

"You did!"

"We were talking, and the next thing I know we were looking into each other's eyes and there was this spark. More like an explosion, really. I felt it before—more than once—and I guess he did, too, because last night he suddenly lays one on me."

"Wow."

"That's exactly how I felt. The kiss… Oh, my goodness, it was amazing. I really don't ever remember feeling that kind of thrill at kissing anyone before. No, I *know* I haven't."

"Could it be you've found your Mr. Right?" Brianne asked in a singsong voice.

Had she? The very thought made Salina's heart pound harder. "I don't know," she said softly. "I feel that he's attracted to me, too—I mean, my attraction is so strong, how can it be one-sided? But already this morning he was avoiding me. This after he spent a full week barely making eye contact with me. That's why I was so surprised when he actually kissed me. But I get the sense that he might be feeling guilty because of his late wife—you know, that he shouldn't be dating because it will be dishonoring her memory. How can I compete with that?"

"You be patient," Brianne told her. "If it's meant to be, it will be. I can tell you as someone who was in love with someone who died—well, *allegedly* died—it can take a while to be ready to move on. For him, it's been a couple of years. If you're right that you're sensing an attraction on his part, he's probably fighting his feelings because he's holding on to his past. But he won't hold on to it forever."

"I think you're right," Salina said.

"If you like him—and it sounds like you do—you've got to be patient. Be there for him, but don't be demanding. That's my best advice for you."

"Thanks. That helps."

At the sound of the door turning, Salina jerked her gaze in that direction. "Speak of the devil, I think he's home. Which is early for him—it's not even five-thirty yet. He spends practically all his time at the office."

"Hmm… Maybe he came home early to spend time with you."

"I've got to go," Salina said hurriedly. "Talk to you later." Then she quickly ended the call.

She was walking back to her purse when Jake entered the apartment. Salina stopped in her tracks. God, he was gorgeous. She knew her heart would always beat a little faster whenever she looked at him.

"Hey," he said softly.

"Hi." Salina crossed her arms over her chest, feeling awkward. When Jake glanced at his sleeping daughter, she said, "Riquet was pooped. She fell asleep, and I was about to make something for dinner. I didn't expect you back so early, so I haven't even started anything."

"No worries," Jake told her. "In fact, I was thinking that maybe we could go out to eat. All three of us."

Salina didn't dare hope. Was he talking about a sort of date? "You—you want all three of us to go out and eat?"

Jake stepped toward her and Salina's breath caught in her throat. Stopping as he reached her, Jake said, "That dinner we had last night was really special. Spending time with Riquet like that. With you. It made me think I need to do more of that. For the longest time, Riquet has been telling me how much she wants to ride a horse. I was thinking that maybe we could head to Central Park and do one of those carriage rides." Jake shrugged. "Maybe eat some hot dogs, or maybe greasy pizza. The kind of thing we never do. I figured Riquet might get a kick out of it. Kind of tacky, I guess, but—"

"No. I don't think that's tacky at all. I think you're right. That's just the kind of thing Riquet will love. She was just telling me today how she would love it if you come to one of her art classes. She really wants to see more of you. So the fact that you're here and wanting to do something with her this evening will make her the happiest little girl in the world."

"I was even thinking that we could head to Rockefeller Center and do some ice skating," Jake concluded.

Salina narrowed her eyes playfully as she looked at Jake. "Don't you have work to do?"

"I always have work to do. But I've also got to make time for my daughter." Jake smiled softly. "You made me realize that."

Salina felt warmth spread through her body. Was Jake really crediting her with his new outlook on life? She was happy to know that she had affected him in such a positive way.

And she couldn't help wondering if Jake was also interested in spending more time with *her*... After all, he could certainly head out with Riquet on his own. He didn't need her to come along in order to spend quality time with his daughter.

She wanted to ask him about the kiss, and if he regretted it. Instead she said, "I don't have any skates here. Well, I don't have any period."

"Neither do I," Jake admitted. "I'm not sure if they rent them out at Rockefeller Center, but if not, we can pick some up at a department store."

"Sounds like a plan."

Jake held her gaze for a long beat, then took a step toward her. Salina was certain that he was going to kiss her again.

"Daddy?"

At the sound of Riquet's voice, Jake halted and quickly turned toward his daughter. Salina released a breath that she didn't realize she had been holding.

"Daddy, you're home!"

Jake headed toward her. "Hey, baby. Yes, Daddy's home. How do you feel about going for a carriage ride in Central Park?"

"Will the horse be white?" Riquet asked, her eyes lighting up.

Jake sat on the sofa beside her. "We'll make sure to pick a carriage with a white horse."

"Yay!" Riquet exclaimed, and threw her arms around her father's neck.

"And then we'll go skating. How does that sound?"

"Skating, too?"

"Yep. We're going to have an evening of fun."

"Is Salina coming, too?" Riquet asked.

Jake looked over his shoulder at Salina. His eyes held hers for a beat before he answered. "Of course. Salina doesn't want to miss out on the fun, do you?"

"Definitely not," Salina said. "I can't wait for the carriage ride."

Riquet beamed, and the happiness she felt spread straight to Salina.

Jake grinned at her, an endearing smile that warmed her heart.

She was falling for this man. Falling for him hard.

Chapter 9

Riquet had to be the happiest little girl in the world. And right now Salina was the happiest woman. She, Jake and Riquet had enjoyed a carriage ride around Central Park, hot dogs and sodas, and now they were at Rockefeller Center's ice rink, ready to enjoy a pastime that many New Yorkers did. They had stopped at a department store to pick up skates, because, as Jake said, that way they could have them for the next time.

Salina had concentrated on the words *next time*. She and Jake had shared some long looks and smiles while taking in the sights like tourists during the carriage ride, and she couldn't help thinking that *next time* held a lot of meaning. Surely, if she was feeling so strongly toward Jake he must be feeling the same toward her.

"I want to ride a horse again," Riquet said to Jake. "But not in a carriage. I want to be on the horse's back. The way Mommy used to be."

"You really want to learn how to ride a horse, huh?" Jake asked his daughter.

"Yes. I want to learn today!"

"Well, it can't be today, honey. But one day soon, okay?"

"When?"

Jake chuckled softly. "Soon. But right now, are you ready to go skating?"

Riquet nodded heartily. "Yes, Daddy."

Jake looked at Salina. "What about you? Are you ready?"

Salina was standing on her skates, but gripping the edge of the rink. She wasn't sure she was ready to join all the people on the ice—people who looked like Olympic medalists compared to her. She didn't want to make a fool of herself.

"I'm not sure," she answered honestly.

"You can do it," Riquet told her. "Watch me."

Holding her father's hand, Riquet ventured onto the ice. Then she let go. She extended her hands at both sides for balance and began to try to move forward on her own. She didn't do too badly at all.

"Come on," Riquet said.

Salina watched as a young boy skated by effortlessly. If that young boy, no more than eight, could do it so well, certainly she could at least give it a try.

Salina moved forward tentatively, taking baby steps. "Oh, goodness," she said, reaching for Jake. "I haven't been on skates in so long."

"Don't worry," Jake told her as he offered her his arm. "I'm here for you to hold on to if you fall."

Despite her fear, Salina looked up at Jake and smiled softly. He was smiling, too, and man did he ever look attractive when he smiled. It was nice to see him enjoying some time with his little girl, as opposed to burying his face in work files all the time.

Riquet took Jake's left hand while Salina held on to his

right arm. Together they inched forward. They moved very slowly, but at least they stayed on their feet as they made their way halfway around the rink.

"See," Jake began, "easy as pie."

"I think I can go by myself," Riquet announced.

"You sure?"

"Uh-huh."

Jake released Riquet's hand slowly, and the little girl moved forward bravely. Though she was stepping as opposed to gliding, she stayed on her feet quite well.

"Oh, for goodness sake, let me give this a real shot," Salina said. She braced herself to let go of Jake's arm, but just as she did, she felt her right foot slip forward. Instinctively, she reached for Jake with both of her hands and gripped him hard—so hard that she caused him to lose his footing. Both of them fell to the ice.

Jake landed on his bottom and Salina's body landed on the hard wall of his chest. For a moment she was stunned. Embarrassed. And then she began to giggle.

Chuckling, as well, Jake slipped his arm around her waist and held her close. And suddenly, what only seconds ago was an awkward moment became an electrically charged one. Salina lay against Jake, watching the condensation that formed as his breath filled the cool air, thinking that his face looked even more handsome as it was bathed in the lights illuminating the ice rink.

"You okay?" he asked her as he gazed deeply into her eyes.

"I'm fine," she told him, the word holding a double meaning for her.

She was more than fine. She was aroused and wanted to kiss him. And given the way he was looking at her, she was certain he wanted the same thing.

But at that moment, his cell phone started to ring, breaking the spell that had gripped both of them. Jake wriggled his body to a sitting position and reached into his pocket and retrieved his BlackBerry. "Hold on one second," he said to whomever was on the line.

Then he worked his way onto his feet. Once he was up, he reached for Salina's hand and pulled her up, too. He put the phone back to his ear. "Hello?"

One moment he had been smiling, the next his face went blank. Salina watched him carefully.

"Oh, man. I completely forgot." He paused. Salina thought she could make out the sound of a woman's voice on the other end of the phone. "I'm at Rockefeller Center with Riquet and the nanny. We're skating." Another pause. "Yes, I know. Don't worry, I'll have Ed come around right now and pick us up."

Jake ended the call and faced Salina. "Everything okay?" she asked.

"That was my mother. She's at my place."

Salina's eyes widened. "She is?"

"Yeah. I completely forgot about a fundraiser for this evening."

"You have to go out?" Salina wasn't ready for their evening together to be so abruptly over.

"Yeah, I do. My father can't make this event, and my mother really wants me to be there with her. I'm sorry."

"No, that's okay." But Salina was disappointed. They had been having a wonderful time together, and once again getting closer. She was certain that he'd wanted to kiss her— even if he wouldn't, given where they were. But her hope had been that once they returned to the apartment, and Riquet was sleeping, maybe they would pick up where they had left off the night before.

Now it looked as though that hope had just been washed down the drain.

* * *

"Grandma!" Riquet ran into the apartment and straight toward the older woman who was sitting on the armchair in the living room. She threw herself onto her grandmother's lap and wrapped her arms around her neck.

"Hello, dear," the woman said, hugging Riquet back for a good, long moment.

Even if Salina had seen this woman in a restaurant instead of Jake's apartment, she would have recognized her as Jake's mother. He looked so much like her, it was uncanny. In fact, Salina would have to guess that Jake had gotten all his looks from his mother's side of the gene pool.

"Hello, Mom," Jake said.

"Evening, Son," she greeted him, but her eyes were on Salina. "Well, who do we have here?"

Riquet slid off her grandmother's lap and bounded toward Salina. "This is my new mommy," Riquet proudly announced.

Now the grandmother's eyes widened—and so did Salina's. Clearly, Riquet had misspoken. *"Nanny,"* Salina quickly said. "She means I'm the new nanny."

Mrs. McKnight rose, her eyes still enlarged. "New nanny?"

"You remember that I told you I was having a temporary nanny to replace Maria," Jake said. "This is her."

"Oh, of course," Jake's mother said. She smiled brightly. "Hello."

Salina approached the woman with her hand extended. "Hello. My name is Salina. Salina Brown."

Mrs. McKnight gave Salina a slow once-over, clearly sizing her up. Then she took Salina's hand and shook it. "I'm Bernice."

She sounded pleasant enough, but Salina wasn't sure she liked the look Jake's mother had given her. There was something disapproving in it. Judgmental. Then again, Jake's mother was clearly surprised to have seen her enter the apartment, and perhaps even a little unhappy that Jake had been off skating with her and Riquet, when he should have been getting ready for this fundraiser.

"Nice to meet you," Salina said.

"Likewise."

Bernice was dressed in an elegant black dress made of silk and lace, that came to below her knees. She wore a single strand of pearls around her neck and her hair was pulled back in a chignon. She had an air of sophistication.

Turning, Bernice walked back into the living room, her movements graceful. She was beautiful, tall and statuesque, with a trim figure. Salina guessed that she was in her mid-to-late fifties, though her flawless dark skin showed no signs of wrinkles.

"Salina has an extensive background in day care," Jake explained. "Her sister works for my law firm, and referred her to me. It's been a great arrangement so far. Riquet really adores her, and she's been an excellent replacement for Maria."

"I see," Bernice said.

Salina smiled politely, but she couldn't help thinking about Jake's words. He had described her role to his mother in a strictly business sense, which Salina knew was true on one hand, but what about their personal relationship? Sure, they weren't dating or anything yet, but Jake may as well have described her as some sort of nanny robot.

"It's an arrangement that's been working out very well."

"Seems like it," Mrs. McKnight said. "She actually had you out skating. That's nice to see…though unfortunately, this was the wrong night for it."

Salina glanced away. She hoped Jake's mother wouldn't be too upset that they would be arriving at the event later than she'd hoped.

"When will Maria return?" his mother went on.

"I don't expect her back before next week," Jake said, "but I wouldn't be surprised if she needed more time. Given her mother's health."

"Well, that's understandable," Bernice said.

"And she's been such an integral part of our lives that I didn't want to deny her the time away. As I said, Salina has been doing an excellent job in her place. And Maria will be back before we know it." As Jake spoke, he ran a hand over his daughter's hair.

Salina couldn't help thinking that Jake was speaking about her with such professional detachment because he was trying extra hard to make his mother not fear that there was anything going on between them. He may as well have added, "And no, don't worry. I didn't kiss her last night. Our arrangement is strictly business."

It annoyed Salina.

Mrs. McKnight glanced at her watch. "Well, I hate to press the issue, but we really need to get going. Thank goodness men can get ready in a fraction of the time it takes women. The silent auction is the first item, and we need to be there for that."

"I'll be quick," Jake said, and headed toward his bedroom.

"How about you stay with your grandmother while I run your bath?" Salina said to Riquet.

"Okay," Riquet agreed.

Salina hustled off down the hallway in the direction of Riquet's bedroom, feeling a little odd. She couldn't help thinking that even though Bernice had been pleasant to her, the woman didn't like her.

Chapter 10

"So tell me about Salina."

At the statement, Jake's heart fluttered. He was in the backseat of his towncar with his mother, and Ed was driving them to the Waldorf Astoria hotel, where tonight's fundraiser was. Tatiana Elliston, a local socialite, was hosting the dinner and auction to raise research money for a rare condition known as Alpers syndrome, a fatal mitochondrial disease that had taken the life of her eighteen-month-old son six years earlier.

"Tell you what?" Jake asked.

"You were out skating with her and Riquet," his mother said, raising an eyebrow. "When was the last time you were on a pair of skates? That trip we took to Vermont when you were fifteen?"

"So?"

"So I'm figuring she has to be something special, if you forgot all about tonight's fundraiser and instead were out enjoying an evening skate. It's a good thing I called you when I did."

"I'm just trying to spend more time with Riquet," Jake explained. "You know how much I've been working lately."

"Of course. Your work ethic will only help you when you finally decide to run for mayor. Hopefully in the next few years," she added, giving him a long look. "But by the same token, you have to remember how important it is to get out to events like this. You need to be involved in the community, have people know your name, so that when you make a run for political office you'll already have support." Bernice paused. "Of course, you know all this."

Jake said nothing. He knew that was his mother's dream, and for a long time it had been his, as well. To work as a lawyer for a number of years, make partner at the firm then leave on a high and enter the political arena. But it had also been a dream he'd shared with his late wife, Janine. And once she'd died, the dream hadn't held much luster.

"You haven't gone to as many events as you once used to," Bernice went on, "but with Janine's untimely passing, that's understandable."

"It wasn't the same without her," Jake said.

"Of course not," Bernice said, her tone laced with sympathy. "No one can fault you for that."

Jake swallowed. He didn't want to think about Janine and that ill-fated night two years ago.

"I have to admit, I was surprised when you came into the apartment with someone so young. After the au pair from England, I thought you would have chosen differently."

"Like I said," Jake began, "her sister works at my firm. That's how I came to know her. I was in a bind, remember? I didn't have all the time in the world to interview people from an agency, and I trust Emma and her opinion. Yes, her sister is young—but she's excellent. Her background in child care is stellar."

"She's quite beautiful." Bernice paused briefly. "And I saw the way she looked at you."

"You saw her for all of five minutes," Jake countered.

"It was enough time."

Jake chuckled without mirth. "Enough time for what?"

"Enough time to see that she's smitten with you."

For some reason, his mother's words made Jake feel irrationally happy. A part of him was excited to think that Salina might be interested in him. But another part of him was terrified about the idea.

His mind ventured to the incredible kiss they had shared last night. He had thought of nothing else for pretty much the entire day. He had a meeting with his partners, and Bill had commented that he seemed distracted.

He *had* been distracted. His mind had replayed the kiss, and that wonderful moment of anticipation before the kiss, over and over again. Salina's lips had looked so soft and delectable. And when they had parted in a soft smile, she had suddenly become irresistible to him. He'd *had* to kiss her. And once he had laid his mouth on hers, he had wanted to do much more.

In the light of day, the reality of the kiss—of his raging desire for her—bothered him on some level. He kept asking himself, why Salina? And why now? He hadn't been looking for love. Indeed, he had resolved to be a single parent and never marry again. He had married and lost the woman he loved, and nothing had been more devastating than that.

But there was something about Salina that made him think that perhaps love was potentially at his door. He wasn't sure how to deal with it.

"I doubt you saw anything like that," Jake said, knowing he wasn't being exactly honest with his mother. Heck, he saw something in Salina's eyes every time he gazed at her. That's the very reason he'd kissed her, something he couldn't tell his mother about. Not the mother who had been so hard on Janine in the early days, and who had only come around to accepting her after a good couple of years. Ultimately, she had become Janine's biggest supporter. And knowing his mother, Jake was certain that she wouldn't like him getting involved with someone else. At least not someone who didn't meet her rigorous standards.

"I want you to be careful, son," Bernice said. "Like I said, she's young, beautiful, and you are a rich and successful man. Women like her will know exactly how to use Riquet to get closer to you."

"Mom, that's out of line."

"Is it? It happens all the time. I'm not saying she doesn't like Riquet, or that she's not good with her—just that she might have her own agenda. How often does an eligible bachelor like you fall from the sky into the life of someone like her?"

Now Jake was becoming irritated. "Mom, you don't even know her. You have no idea what her background is, what her life has been like."

"And I'm sorry if I'm coming off as harsh. I just want you to consider that you have a lot more to lose if things go wrong. Like I said, she seems like a nice girl, but nice girls have agendas, too."

Jake said nothing. Why bother to belabor the point with his mother?

"I'm sorry," Bernice said. "I can see I've upset you."

Jake rubbed his temples. He loved his mother, and didn't like conflict with her. All of his life he had done his best to not upset her, because he knew she had his best interests at heart. "There's a lot going on in my life, Mom. With that class-action lawsuit and my work schedule, the last thing on my mind is love and romance and being taken advantage of by some girl who has an agenda."

"I *have* upset you," Bernice said.

"It's just that sometimes I think you don't give me enough credit for having a brain in my head," Jake told her.

"I'm sorry," Bernice said. "I know you're smart. I'm not saying that. I guess—I guess I was just thinking you might be vulnerable. And I would understand that. Because it's been two years since we lost Janine. I couldn't blame you for wanting some companionship."

Was that the basis for Jake's attraction to Salina? Simply the fact that Jake was lonely and missing the companionship of a woman? Was that why kissing her had set his body on fire? Why a part of him that had died had come screaming back to life?

"I'm too busy to be vulnerable," Jake told his mother, knowing that that was exactly what he had done. Made himself excessively busy as a way to avoid feeling pain.

But there was something about Salina, something that was soft and sweet, and so feminine and beautiful that she touched him on a primal level. It was more than the fact that she was great with Riquet, which certainly helped endear her to him. There was something about her that spoke to him as a man.

Jake looked forward as Ed navigated the streets of New York. Thick snowflakes were falling from the sky. He remembered the grin on Riquet's face as she'd looked up at the sky and stuck her tongue out to catch some flakes while they'd been on the carriage ride earlier. He wanted to be home with her tonight, tuck her into bed for a change.

And then spend time with Salina once Riquet was asleep.

"Ah, here we are," Bernice said as the Waldorf Astoria hotel came into view.

It was certainly a beautiful hotel, and Jake had enjoyed spending the occasional night here with Janine in the past.

"Come on, son," Bernice said. "Let's head inside."

She had a twinkle in her eye that made Jake's nape tingle. He suddenly wondered if she was up to something.

Jake and his mother entered the lavishly decorated ball-room a short while later. Around the perimeter of three walls in the room were tables on which were displayed the various items for the silent auction. The room was filled with happy chatter. The women were attired in gorgeous cocktail dresses and the men in tailored suits. Most were holding champagne flutes as they wandered the room.

Jake walked toward the first display table, not particularly feeling the vibe of the event, but willing to purchase something in order to support the cause. No one should have to lose a child the way Tatiana had.

After several minutes of perusing the items on the tables, Jake glanced around the room, figuring it was time to start mingling, as his mother was.

He turned—and that's when he got an inkling of what his mother might be up to.

Elizabeth Dumont, his former girlfriend from another lifetime, was in the room, standing about fifteen feet away from him and talking to two well-dressed older men.

Jake could never forget that long, graceful neck and her beautiful hourglass figure. Tonight she was wearing a form-fitting, over-the-shoulder black dress that hugged her body, emphasizing her shapely form. Her shoulder-length black hair was swept up in a chignon.

Suddenly his mother was at his side. "Ah, look who's here," she said brightly. "Elizabeth Dumont."

For a moment, Jake let himself remember what it had been like to date Elizabeth. That was all he needed. A moment.

Dating Elizabeth had been fine for the time, but it wasn't something he wanted to do again.

No matter what his mother might have up her sleeve.

"Mother," Jake said tightly. "What are you up to?"

"What?" Bernice asked innocently.

Jake knew better. "You know what I'm talking about."

His mother looked him in the eye. "Maybe it's time you start dating again."

Jake stared at her in disbelief. "What are you talking about? You spent the car ride over here telling me that I shouldn't be thinking about dating. You gave me that whole lecture about Salina."

"Perhaps I'm not making myself clear. I don't mean you should start dating Salina. Heavens no. What I mean is that maybe it's time you start dating someone who can help advance your political career."

Jake was baffled. "Someone like Elizabeth," he supplied. "That's why you wanted me at this event with you, isn't it?"

"I ran into her the other day at a dinner in Charlotte," his mother said, not answering his question. "She's volunteering with Organizing For America—the organization that supports the current administration—"

"I know what it is," Jake said testily. "What I want to know is if you asked me to come to this event because of Elizabeth."

"She asked about you," Bernice said simply.

"I'm sure she did."

Despite the fact that they hadn't dated in over eight years, Elizabeth still held a torch for him. She seemed unable to accept the fact that he had broken up with her, met Janine and ultimately proposed to Janine, when she'd always believed that he would marry her.

And while Jake hadn't cheated on Elizabeth, he hadn't told her the true order of events. He'd still been dating Elizabeth when he met Janine and felt an immediate and strong connection to her, so much so that he knew he could no longer date Elizabeth. He broke up with Elizabeth, started dating Janine, was engaged within three months and married six months after that. To spare Elizabeth's feelings—because she had taken the breakup badly—Jake hadn't told her that he'd left her because he'd met someone else with whom he'd had an instant connection.

Jake remembered the last time Elizabeth had run into him while he was married, about four months before Janine's death. She had come on to him ruthlessly, as though he were single, begging him for one more night of pleasure for old time's sake. Jake had lost all respect for her then.

"She shouldn't be asking about me when she's engaged," Jake said to his mother.

"You haven't heard? She called off the engagement."

Jake would bet that her fiancé had called off the engagement—once the man had learned about her flirtatious ways.

Jake glanced in Elizabeth's direction again, and this time he found her looking at him. She raised her champagne flute in greeting. He waved back.

"I'm not sure I feel like sticking around," he suddenly said.

"Organizing For America is an excellent group, a very worthy cause. The kind of cause that can certainly help your future ambitions. She might just be a perfect wife for you."

"Wife?"

"You dated her before Janine—"

"And I left her for a reason." Jake gritted his teeth. While he'd been dating her, Elizabeth had displayed a nasty jealous side, which only made it easier to leave her, once he had met Janine.

"You were both young then," Bernice said. "Both a little immature."

"*I* was immature?"

"Enough time has passed now that she's grown up. I'm certain she's past her jealousy. And what harm would it do to get to know her again?"

Jake wondered why his mother was suddenly pushing this issue. One minute she was telling him that he shouldn't be dating, the next she was practically throwing him into Elizabeth's path.

"So you met my new nanny and suddenly you think I need to be dating. Why—to make sure I don't get involved with Salina?"

His mother didn't answer right away. But slowly she nodded. "Yes. I met her, saw the way she looked at you, and it made me realize that a man like you needs a wife. You don't want to have people look at you and assume you're sleeping with your hired help. If you're involved with someone else, making the rounds regularly at events with another woman, well, that can only help your image."

"A woman like Elizabeth?" Jake asked.

"Yes, a woman like Elizabeth. What's wrong with her?"

Jake didn't answer. His mother didn't know about how Elizabeth had tried to seduce him while he had been married to Janine. Elizabeth might be fine for another man— someone who cared more about looks than a person's moral fiber.

But even assuming that his mother was right and Elizabeth had matured, Jake was over her. He wasn't in love with her, and he found no point in rehashing his old relationship with her, just to keep up appearances for the sake of a political career he might pursue.

A career Jake wasn't all that interested in anymore. He was starting to realize that people in public office simply didn't have the kind of freedom that he desired. It was a part of the reason that he had ducked out from the social scene after Janine's death.

If people wanted to be suspicious of everything he did, let them. Hadn't he had enough of the walk-on-eggshells lifestyle when he was a child? His father had been first a popular minister who had successfully moved on to city politics, and then to state politics. Because of his father's own political career, his parents had expected that he would also enter the political arena and they had spent their lives preparing him to do so.

"Perhaps it's fate that she's here tonight," Bernice said. "I think it would be worth your time to talk with her."

Jake narrowed his eyes at his mother. Then he looked in Elizabeth's direction again, saw her casting sidelong glances at him. "You should've told me why you really wanted me here."

"Talk to her, son."

Clenching his jaw, Jake once again looked at Elizabeth. She met his gaze and smiled brightly at him. He knew that she was aware of her good looks. Aware of how men reacted to her. Her skin was the complexion of café au lait, and still flawless from what he could tell. She had bright eyes and long lashes. She knew just how to accentuate her features with makeup to make herself look even better. Granted, she didn't need any makeup to make herself look good.

Yes, like other men, Jake had initially been attracted to her beauty, as well. As he'd gotten to know her, however, he had learned that there was a shallowness to her.

Perhaps shallow wasn't the perfect word. She did charity work, gave back to the less fortunate. But it all felt a little superficial to him. That, coupled with her jealous streak, had ensured they would have no future.

Elizabeth made her way through the crowd, approaching

him. She walked gracefully, as if on air. "Hello, Jake," she purred when she reached him.

Jake glanced at his mother, saw her beaming. He wondered what his mother found so appealing about Elizabeth—other than her connections. Elizabeth's father was a powerful senator in North Carolina. That was the kind of connection that would only help Jake's future political career. That was what mattered to his mother.

"Hello," Jake said.

Elizabeth greeted his mother, then leaned forward to kiss her on the cheek before turning her attention back to Jake. "Good to see you again," she said to him. She linked her arm through his. "I'm glad you could make it."

"Good turnout," Jake said.

Elizabeth nodded. "Yes. I'm so pleased for Tatiana. I'm certain a large sum of money will be raised for the cause."

Bernice spoke then. "Oh, I see your father," she said to Elizabeth. "I'm going to go say hi."

And try to secure his support for the yet to be determined political career of your son, Jake thought sourly.

Maybe Jake was in a foul mood because these events reminded him of Janine. She had thoroughly enjoyed them, and without her, these events seemed hollow somehow. Janine had shared his mother's goal that Jake enter politics, and at the time, Jake had believed that yes, perhaps one day he would take a run for mayor, and then beyond. Now, seeing this roomful of people who had mostly stayed away after his wife died, he couldn't help feeling bitter toward them.

Were they really his friends? Where had they been during the worst time of his life?

Elizabeth stayed close to Jake's side as he wandered the room and greeted people, then as he went back to peruse the items up for auction.

"This is stunning," Elizabeth said as she looked at a multicolored necklace made of Austrian crystal.

If Elizabeth hoped he would bid on it for her, she had another thought coming.

Jake was starting to believe that he wouldn't bid on anything—until he saw the cookware set a few feet away.

He walked toward it. It was an all-clad, copper-core, fourteen-piece cookware set designed by one of New York's most popular chefs, Donald Martin. Jake thought of Salina immediately. Wondered if she had a designer cookware set like this.

The current high bid on the sheet of paper was one thousand two hundred dollars. Jake scribbled his name on the next line, and the amount of twenty-five-hundred dollars.

"Planning to do some cooking?" Elizabeth asked him.

"Something like that," Jake answered.

Elizabeth continued to walk by his side, and much to Jake's dismay she was seated at his table for dinner. Something his mother likely not only knew about ahead of time, but probably arranged.

Jake could only hope that Elizabeth wasn't getting any deluded ideas in her head that he might be interested in picking up where they had left off eight years ago. They were friends. They could talk and hang out at an event. Certainly she wouldn't read more into things than that.

But when Jake was exiting the bathroom a couple of hours later, he was surprised to see Elizabeth standing there. Looking up at him, she smiled, making it clear she had been waiting for him.

"Elizabeth—"

She stepped forward and put a finger against his lips. "Don't say anything."

And then she eased up on her toes and kissed him on the lips.

Jake backed away from her. "Elizabeth—"

"Don't be mad at me," she said. "I just wanted to see if I still felt something."

Jake said nothing, just wiped his mouth with the back of his hand. He wasn't going to entertain her fantasies. He wasn't going to support her delusions. Any relationship that he and Elizabeth could've ever had was ancient history.

"Don't you want to know what I felt?" she asked, giving him a coy look.

"I'm heading back to the table."

As Jake stepped past her, Elizabeth said, "I felt something. Didn't you?"

"No," Jake told her frankly.

Elizabeth chuckled softly, as though she couldn't believe what he'd said. "You should call me sometime. We should get together for lunch."

"Enough, Elizabeth," Jake said firmly.

And then he stalked past her, back into the ballroom.

When Elizabeth took a seat beside him minutes later, and he saw his mother's eyebrows rise in interest, Jake realized what she must be thinking. Perhaps even what others might be speculating. He had been missing from the table. So had Elizabeth. People were no doubt thinking that he and Elizabeth had just sneaked off for some romantic time.

But the only thing Jake was thinking was that right now he wanted to be kissing Salina. He wanted to feel her lips against his again. Elizabeth kissing him minutes earlier had made that all the more clear to him.

He *had* given in to his desire for Salina last night, and then spent the day rationalizing it away. Still, he had been compelled to head home from work early and spend more time with her. He had tried to deny his feelings for Salina because he felt a measure of respect for Janine that he shouldn't go there.

But suddenly, right here at this dinner table, he was feeling a desire for Salina so profound that he knew he couldn't stay here any longer.

He turned to his mother. "I have to leave."

She stared at him in shock. "But you haven't eaten your dinner."

He had eaten dinner. A big, juicy hot dog in Times Square. "I'm not hungry," he told her. "And I have files to go through before tomorrow. Don't worry—you stay and enjoy the event. I'll have Ed come back and pick you up."

When he pushed his chair back, Elizabeth placed her hand on his arm. "Jake?"

"Good night, Elizabeth." He spoke the words with finality, hoping to put to rest her fantasy that they might ever get involved again.

And then Jake headed out the door, excited about going home and seeing Salina.

Chapter 11

Back at his apartment, Jake went straight to Salina's door and knocked softly. It was late—after ten—but he could hear the sound of the television playing inside the room.

Jake swallowed. Then he raised his hand and knocked on the door.

There was a pause, and then he heard Salina's voice. "Jake?"

He turned the door handle and opened the door a crack, but didn't step inside. "Yes," he said. "It's me."

"Come in," Salina called softly.

Jake did so, and found Salina standing up in the middle of the room, as though she had been en route to the door. Wearing a terry cloth robe that was knotted around her waist, she was looking at him curiously. Perhaps she was wondering why he was home so early, or wondering why he had come to the room to see her.

"The event is already finished?" she asked.

"I don't want to talk about the event," Jake told her.

"No?"

Jake shook his head as he stepped forward. "No."

Salina's eyes widened as Jake moved toward her. He wasted no time pulling her into his arms and kissing her. Salina stiffened against him, clearly shocked at what was happening. But moments later he felt her resistance ebb away. She softened against him, her curves melting into him. He groaned and dragged his fingers through her softly curled hair, tightening his hold on her as his lips ravaged hers.

They kissed like that, all fire and passion, until Salina stepped backward and stared up at him. She was confused. He could see it in her eyes. "What… What was that?"

Jake took a step toward her and she took a step backward. "I kissed you."

"I know that. What I want to know is why."

Why indeed? All Jake knew was that he had wanted this, whether he had accepted it on a conscious level or not. He wanted to taste her lips again, determine if they were as sweet as he remembered they were from the night before.

"I needed to kiss you," he said.

Salina looked skeptical. "Are you sure? After all, I'm only the nanny."

So she was upset because of what he'd said to his mother. "Yes, I'm sure."

"You didn't seem so sure when your mother was here."

"How can I tell my mother what I am feeling when I don't even understand it myself? The truth is, I haven't wanted another woman since Janine died. But you…"

Silence fell between them. Jake wondered if Salina was upset that he'd mentioned his late wife. So he was surprised when she was the one to take a step toward him.

"Do that again," she said. "Let me know I'm not dreaming this right now."

Jake smiled. And then he took her in his arms, framed

her face gently and kissed her. He kissed her until she was panting with need. She sagged against him as her soft lips mated with his, and Jake had to hold her up.

Jake broke the kiss and stared at her. He saw the need in her eyes, a need that matched what he was feeling.

"Do you still feel like you're dreaming?"

"Yes," Salina said softly. "But in a good way, because I know I'm very much awake."

"I want to make love to you," he told her bluntly.

He saw her eyes widen, and, God, wasn't she incredibly beautiful? He caressed her face with his fingers and kissed her again, a softer kiss, but one still filled with passion and need.

When he broke the kiss, Salina said to him, "No. Please don't pull away from me. I—I want you, too."

Jake planted his lips on hers again and wrapped his arms around her waist. He pulled her tightly against him. She slipped her arms around his neck and tipped up on her toes as she purred into his mouth.

Oh, how that soft sound, that wonderfully soft sound full of need, drove Jake crazy. He lifted Salina and she wrapped her legs around his waist. Unable to take his mouth off hers, he kissed her like that for several seconds, then walked with her to her nearby bed.

Salina gripped him tighter. Reaching the edge of the mattress, Jake put a knee down on the bed and eased Salina onto her back. He took her hands in his and stretched her arms out over her head. He pulled his lips from hers only to kiss the underside of her jaw.

"Oh, my goodness," Salina said as his tongue worked along her skin. "That feels so good…."

He brought his hands down and smoothed them over her torso. She was wearing a robe—one that was in the way.

Easing upward, Jake hurriedly loosened the obstructing garment.

And then he met her eyes. Even in the darkness of the room he could see that they were shimmering with desire. The blinds were open, allowing moonlight to spill into the bedroom. The vision of Salina on the bed, ready to make love with him, made his breath catch.

He wanted this. But he had to make sure that she wanted it, too. "Are you sure?"

In response to his question, Salina sat up and pulled the robe off her body. All she wore now was an oversize T-shirt.

Nothing had looked as sexy on a woman. No lace bra, no thong underwear—absolutely nothing.

"I'm sure," she told him.

Jake pressed his mouth to hers again, and her soft moans turned him on more than ever. He felt like a man about to make love to a woman for the very first time.

As he kissed her, his hands moved to her breasts. He stroked the sides through the fabric of her T-shirt, groaning in pleasure when he felt no bra there. Of course she wasn't wearing a bra. She had been dressed for bed.

Salina arched her back, pushing her breasts against his hands. He knew she wanted him to touch her more intimately.

He wanted that, too.

So he moved his hand from the side of her breast and to her nipple. Her long, rapturous moan was his reward. His groin tightened, and he could no longer stand that she had clothes on her body. He pushed her T-shirt up and over her breasts, and then immediately brought his mouth down onto one of her hardened peaks.

She flinched beneath him, cried out in ecstasy. He twirled his tongue around her nipple and suckled her until she was moaning relentlessly.

He needed more of her. All of her.

We'd like to send you two free books to introduce you to Kimani™ Romance books. These novels feature strong, sexy women, and African-American heroes that are charming, loving and true. Our authors fill each page with exceptional dialogue, exciting plot twists, and enough sizzling romance to keep you riveted until the very end!

KIMANI ROMANCE...LOVE'S ULTIMATE DESTINATION

Your two books have combined cover pric of $12.50 in the U.S. $14.50 in Canada, bu are yours **FREE!**

We'll even send you two wonderful surprise gifts. You can't lose!

2 FREE BONUS GIFTS!

absolutely FREE

Quickly, he pulled her panties off her body and tossed them onto the floor. Then he reached into the jacket pocket of his blazer and pulled out the small package of condoms he had picked up downstairs at a convenience store before he had come up to his apartment.

Salina was still moaning as he took off his jacket, his dress shirt, and then slipped out of his pants. As he pulled off his briefs, she sat up. He saw her eyes take in every inch of him. And then he did the same as she pulled the T-shirt over her head and tossed it aside.

She was lovely. Absolutely stunning. Perfect small breasts, a narrow waist and rounded hips he wanted to smooth his hands over. The center of her womanhood was a vision of sheer beauty. Good Lord, she was spectacular.

Jake tore open the condom wrapper. It took him longer than he wanted to get the thing on, but he succeeded. It had been a while.

He was about to rectify that.

He moved forward and eased over her body, his mouth coming down onto hers hard. His body was on fire with need.

Jake covered one of her breasts and tweaked the nipple as he slipped his tongue into her mouth. With his other hand, he guided her knees apart and settled between her thighs.

Salina emitted a breathy moan, and Jake needed no further encouragement. She was ready for him, and he entered her with a hard thrust.

And, Good Lord, the sensations. Had he ever felt this incredible?

But he couldn't savor the feeling, not when he realized that Salina had gone still. Was she regretting her decision to make love?

"Jake..." She sounded breathless. "It's been so long, and, ohhh...this feels so good."

Jake grinned, relieved. Salina kissed his neck and dug her fingers into his back, urging him to go on.

Jake began to make love to her slowly, enjoying every exquisite moment. Salina hugged him tightly, moved against him urgently, wanting this as much as he did. And soon his body was on sensory overload.

It had been two years, two long years in which Jake had mistakenly believed he could live out the rest of his days without the touch of a woman. But it was all too clear just how much he had missed touching a woman, kissing a woman….

Making love to a woman.

And not just any woman. He was glad that it was Salina in his arms now.

In his bed.

His need for her was all-consuming. Something about her spoke to him at his core. He was crazy about her, even if he didn't understand it.

He knew that he could stay here with her like this, making love to her for hours, and never want the morning to come.

And now that he'd had a taste of her… He kissed her deeply as their bodies moved together faster, knowing that one taste would never be enough.

Jake felt Salina's body quiver beneath his and knew that her release was coming. And that's when he allowed himself to let go.

He went over the edge with her, into a fiery abyss of pleasure that consumed them both.

Salina lay on her bed in a state of wonder.

Had she really just made love to Jake?

She rolled onto her side, stretching her arm over the warm spot where Jake's body had been only minutes before. It was shortly after midnight, and he'd told her that it was best he head to his own room to sleep, in case Riquet awoke in the night.

Salina hadn't argued. She had hardly been able to find her voice. She still couldn't believe that Jake had just made love to her.

She replayed the night's events in her mind. Jake knocking on her bedroom door. Jake entering her room. Jake sweeping her into his arms and kissing her senseless before she'd known what was going on.

Salina's naked body flushed at the memory. She felt incredible. Never before had she ever experienced the kind of hot passion that she'd felt with Jake. He was a phenomenal lover.

She rolled onto her back, sighing contentedly. She wasn't sure what had come over him, but certainly come tomorrow, he wouldn't be avoiding her anymore.

Would he?

Salina bit down on her bottom lip as a smile spread on her face. A part of her was tempted to get out of bed, walk naked to Jake's room and initiate round two.

But she could wait until tomorrow, couldn't she? She could wait for a second delicious taste of him.

Salina thought of her friend Brianne's words. Brianne had told her that if Jake was interested in her, then all he needed was time. Salina had agreed that being patient was the best course of action.

That had been her plan. Then Jake had entered her bedroom, patience the last thing on his mind.

Tonight had proved that he wasn't holding back anymore. He had loved his wife, lost her and was now ready to move on.

He was ready to move on with *her*.

And Salina couldn't be happier.

Chapter 12

Jake wasn't distant the next morning, but he was hardly the amorous lover Salina had hoped he would be. Perhaps because Riquet was awake and in the kitchen as Salina prepared breakfast, and he didn't want his daughter to pick up on the fact that anything had changed between him and her nanny. Salina understood that, but she definitely hoped that Jake would slip her a kiss on the cheek—do *something*—when Riquet wasn't looking.

He didn't.

After he left for work, Salina was back to feeling uncertain about him. Had he made love to her in a moment of need but now regretted it?

She decided she would talk to him. When he got home, after Riquet was asleep, she would sit down and have a heart-to-heart with him.

But Salina got the disappointing news from Jake later that day that he had to leave town. Something had come up suddenly, and he would be gone for two to three days.

"But what about your clothes?" Salina asked him. "What about toiletries?"

"I'm going to have to pick stuff up when I get to Dallas," Jake explained. "The firm will bill the client."

"But—but—" Salina sputtered.

"I can't talk now," Jake told her, putting an end to their short conversation. "I'll call later."

But later, when he called, Jake sounded exhausted, and after saying good-night to Riquet, Salina thought it best not to have a talk with him about the status of their relationship.

In fact, she figured it best not to have this discussion over the phone, and decided she'd be better off waiting for Jake to return.

But by the time Friday rolled around, Salina was back to feeling insecure. Her conversations with Jake had been brief and infrequent, causing her to believe that he wasn't interested in discussing what had happened between them— which ultimately had her believing that he regretted their making love.

Jake was exhausted when his plane touched down at JFK Airport. He also felt anxious—anxious about seeing Salina again.

His work had taken him to Dallas for depositions with regards to the class-action lawsuit, and he had been extremely busy during his time away. Salina had been in his thoughts so much the first day, he realized he had to try to put her out of his mind so that she wouldn't be a distraction.

It had been all but impossible to forget about their mind-blowing lovemaking. Jake's only regret was that he hadn't taken the kind of time with her he would have liked, partly because Riquet was in the apartment and partly because his need had been so explosive, given just how long it had been since he'd last made love.

And while he'd been away from her, Jake found himself contemplating exactly why he was attracted to her. Some things you couldn't explain, and perhaps this was one of them. But he had decided to keep their contact to a minimum for the days he was away, as an experiment. He wanted to see if less contact between them would somehow purge her from his system.

Instead, as Jake's car pulled up to his building, he was more excited than ever to see her. Clearly, time and distance were not going to change his attraction to her.

Shortly after 6:00 p.m., he inserted the key into the lock and stepped into the apartment. Riquet, who was sprawled on the living room floor with her art kit in front of her, saw him immediately. She leaped to her feet and ran toward him.

"Daddy!" Riquet threw herself into his arms.

Jake scooped her up and twirled her around. "Hey, sweetheart. I missed you so much!"

"I missed you more!"

"Where's Salina?"

Just then, Salina rounded the corner from the kitchen, a guarded expression on her face. She was drying her hands on a dish towel.

After a moment, she offered him a weak smile. "You're back."

"Yeah, I'm back."

She nodded, her expression grim. Jake figured she had to be unhappy because of how little they had communicated. He had made himself keep his distance as a test of his feelings for her. And now he knew that he truly was attracted to her, not just lonely because he had been single for so long.

Just one look at her and his heart was already beating faster.

"I only made a pizza," Salina began. "And a small one at that, since I didn't know when you were coming back."

"No worries," Jake told her. "I didn't expect anything."

"I can cook something for you, if you like," she told him. "There's salmon in the freezer. It won't take too long to defrost."

"Don't worry about me. I'll order something."

Salina paused, stared at him. Then she glanced away. "Um, are you planning to work tomorrow?"

"As a matter of fact, no. I've put in more than enough hours for this week."

"So you won't need me?"

The question stumped Jake. "You—you want to leave for the weekend?"

"If you don't need me...I kind of figured..."

"You've put in a lot of hours this week, too."

Salina said nothing, just wrung her fingers together. Jake gave Riquet a quick peck on the cheek and then lowered her to the ground. "If you want some time to yourself, sure, you can leave." Salina didn't speak, and Jake slowly approached her. He held her gaze, steady and strong. "But I'd really like it if you stayed."

Her eyes widened slightly, then narrowed with skepticism. "You want me to stay?" She sounded dubious.

"I—yes—" He stopped abruptly, considering what to say. His first thought was to tell her that he wanted her to stay for Riquet, but he had just acknowledged that she was deserving of some time off. Besides, that would be a lie. He wanted her to stay for his sake.

"I was thinking that maybe we could do something tomorrow," he said, deciding to be honest. He had been thinking about that as he had flown back to New York. He had enjoyed their time on the carriage ride and skating so much that he wanted to create another memory like that. For Riquet, for Salina and for him.

"Something like what?"

"Something fun. All three of us."

Salina looked surprised and Jake couldn't blame her. He knew he had been up and down where she was concerned. One minute he was kissing her, making love to her and generally letting his guard down. The next he was putting up the wall he'd been so accustomed to since losing his wife.

But how did he deal with the feelings he was having for Salina? It wasn't as simple as saying, "I like you. Let's sail off into the sunset together." As attracted as he was to her, he didn't want to rush headlong into a new relationship.

He did want to continue to get to know her—and sharing more experiences was the way to do that.

She had come into his life out of the blue, and he hadn't planned to feel anything for her. Shockingly, he *did* feel something—and he had been conflicted over those feelings in the past few days. On one hand he didn't regret making love to Salina. Not at all. On the other hand he felt a measure of guilt.

It was just that his feelings for Salina had developed very quickly. And his rational brain told him that was wrong. That it should take him months to develop feelings for another woman after how deeply he had loved Janine.

But he knew that even Janine wouldn't want him to sit around pining for her, holding on to what they'd had and not moving on. There was no point in that. She was never coming back.

"We could go horseback riding," Jake said. For the longest time, Riquet had been asking if she could take riding lessons. Jake felt she was too young—but he had also refrained from giving in to the idea, because horse riding had been Janine's passion. Taking Riquet for lessons would have been yet another painful reminder of all that Jake had lost.

"You want to go horseback riding?" Salina asked, sounding as though she didn't believe him.

Or as if she was unhappy with him. She wasn't easily warming to his suggestion of spending more time together.

Jake was glad that he'd decided to leave the package he'd picked up for her en route from the airport in the car. Now wasn't the time to surprise her with the gift. Tomorrow, if they had a great day, he could give it to her then.

"People go horseback riding at this time of year?" Salina went on.

"I have a friend who's got a place in the country. In fact, it's one of my clients for whom I'm working on the class-action lawsuit I told you about. He said that any time I wanted to bring Riquet to his place to do some horseback riding, I was welcome. He's got a huge farm and equestrian center—horses are a big part of his life. I'm up for the adventure if you are."

"And you want to go tomorrow?" Salina asked for clarification.

"If you have nothing better to do." Jake smiled softly.

He could see the conflicted emotions in Salina's eyes. It was all the more reason for them to get out of the city and do something together. Spend more time together and determine if they were really developing a relationship that would last—as opposed to one based on lust.

"Have you already spoken to him?" Salina asked. "Isn't tomorrow too short notice?"

"I can call. Find out."

He thought that he detected a spark in Salina's eyes for the first time since he had arrived home. It was a spark that made him feel warm all over. Because it told him that she was happy about the idea of spending more time with him, as well.

"I guess there's nothing specific I have to do at home. I was figuring I could hang out with my sister for a bit, but she'll probably be out with her boyfriend—if not putting in extra hours on a case."

"So I should call Baxter?" Jake asked.

"Okay," she said, and flashed a little grin.

"Good. I'll call and ask him right away."

Jake went to his bedroom, withdrew his BlackBerry from his jacket pocket and found the contact information for Baxter, the wealthy rancher who'd suffered life-threatening side effects after taking the medication for asthma. Jake knew he was acting out of character by making the call, because he normally believed that you should give a person a decent amount of notice before expecting to plan something like this. And yet he didn't want Salina to leave. If that meant arranging something last minute so that she could stay, then that was what he was going to do.

Minutes later he was triumphant when Baxter told him that they were free to come to his property the next day, no problem, because he would be there all day to cater to them.

Jake went back out to the living room and told Salina the good news. "It's a date," he said. "We're going horseback riding."

"Horseback riding?" Riquet asked, her eyes brightening.

"Yep." Jake grinned at his daughter. "You, me and Salina are taking a trip to a big equestrian center tomorrow. And we're going to enjoy riding horses all day."

And tomorrow, after their day together, he would surprise Salina with the gift he'd bought for her. The cookware set he'd won at the silent auction.

Salina was sitting in the passenger seat of Jake's late-model black Cadillac Escalade the next morning as they drove toward Cortlandt Manor, an area about ninety minutes north of New York City, where Jake's client had his farm and equestrian center. She was so used to Ed driving her around that it was odd to see Jake at the wheel.

For the first twenty minutes, Riquet had chatted excitedly about how she was going to ride on the biggest horse at the farm. Then she had fallen silent as she watched the Tinkerbell movie playing on her portable DVD player. Salina, who had never been on a horse before, was frightened somewhat about riding one—but she was more frightened about the idea that she and Jake were spending time together, because she didn't know what it meant.

Her thought last night, when he'd asked her to stick around, was that he'd quickly invented an idea for her to stay. But did he want her around simply because of how well she interacted with his daughter? Or did he want her around for *her*?

After making love to him, she wished she knew the answer to that question. But the truth was Salina had no idea what to think. Heck, maybe Jake only wanted her to tag along so that he could create a family experience for his daughter.

And yet, as she sat next to him in his vehicle, that explanation didn't quite ring true. Something about this particular outing felt more like she and Jake were taking a step toward perhaps starting a new relationship.

It was the way he kept giving her little looks—looks that she would swear held meaning. Yes, it had been a while since she had dated, but she couldn't be that way off-base when it came to judging a man's attraction to her.

Could she?

"So," Salina began, shortly after they merged onto I-87 North. She wanted to live in the moment, not think about the future. As Brianne had said, Jake could still need time. She had no idea what he was going through emotionally. "You didn't say if you've ridden a horse before. Have you?"

Jake nodded. "I used to take lessons when I was a kid."

"So you're a pro," Salina said.

Jake chuckled softly. "I'm no equestrian," he said, "but I can hold my own. At least I did *waaay* back in the day. Time will tell how I do now. In about another hour, we'll see if I still have what it takes."

"Daddy used to like to watch me and Mommy ride," Riquet said from the backseat. She had been absorbed in her movie, so Salina was surprised to hear her contribute to the conversation. Clearly, the young girl had been paying attention.

Riquet often talked about things she'd done with her mother, things Salina was certain she was too young to have remembered, given that she was only two when her mother died. Jake had obviously kept his late wife's memory alive by telling Riquet lots of stories about her. Riquet's love of horses seemed to stem from Janine's love of horses and riding.

Salina glanced at Jake, hoping to gauge his reaction to the mention of his late wife. But he didn't look at her. He kept his eyes on the road.

Salina's heart sank somewhat. She didn't want to think about Jake's late wife, but more so, she didn't want him thinking of her when they were about to enjoy the day together. Obviously, Janine had been a big part of Jake's life and he would never forget her—Salina just didn't want her coming between them today.

The problem was, one minute Salina and Jake were getting close, the next he was pulling away. There was only one reason for that that made any sense.

The fact that Janine was still in Jake's thoughts.

But was she also still in his heart?

And if she was, was there any room left in Jake's heart for him to love someone else?

Chapter 13

"**I** can't believe you've never been on a horse before," Riquet said to Salina when they arrived at Sunny Trails Farms an hour later. The place didn't look like any type of farm Salina had ever seen before. In fact, the large, sprawling property, complete with a massive white dome, looked like an elaborate complex.

"Well, I've been on a pony before," Salina explained. "The kind you find at a fair. But I know that's not the same."

"I hope you don't fall off!" Riquet exclaimed, giggling a little.

"Riquet," Jake said in a mildly scolding tone, as he put his vehicle in park in front of the white dome structure, "that's not very nice."

"It's fine," Salina said. "She has a good point—and every reason to be concerned. I may just fall off."

"If you fall off I'll catch you," Jake said.

Salina's breath caught in her throat at the simple statement. Slowly she turned—a little scared to look at Jake at that moment because she didn't want to read anything into his words. But when she looked into his eyes, he held her gaze for a long beat. And something passed between them. An electric charge. Real and strong.

Salina had told herself not to get her hopes up where Jake was concerned, that it could be months, years—or never—before he was ready for another relationship. But with that look he gave her, she was back to hoping, back to welcoming the feelings that were quickly developing for this man.

Jake looked away first, glancing forward. Salina saw that a man had exited the dome building and was waving as he walked toward them. The man was tall, well over six-foot-four it seemed, and he was wearing a cowboy hat, cowboy boots and a white goose-down jacket. He had to be Baxter.

Jake opened the car door and exited. He grinned as he walked toward the man and shook his hand.

"Glad you could make it," Salina could hear Baxter saying.

"Thanks for having us," Jake replied.

Salina exited the vehicle and went to the backseat, where she unbuckled Riquet from her car seat. She helped her out of the car.

By the time she looked up, Baxter was approaching her, hand outstretched. "You must be Salina."

Salina shook his hand. "Hello, Baxter."

Baxter bent over to greet Riquet. "And you must be Riquet." He smiled warmly at her. "You're just as pretty as your daddy said you were."

Riquet leaned closer to Salina's leg, but grinned shyly at Baxter. "Thank you."

"How was the drive up?" Baxter asked as Jake came around to their side of the car.

"It was great. The roads were clear, the sky cloudless."

"It was very scenic," Salina added. "All this clean, white snow covering the trees…it's quite picturesque."

"That's why I love it out here," Baxter said, grinning.

"Can we ride a horse now?" Riquet asked.

"Absolutely," Baxter replied. "Follow me."

"Oh, my God. Oh, my God," Salina was whimpering over and over again. She was holding the horse's reins and Jake was walking alongside her, with his hand perched on her back for extra safety. She had chosen one of the smaller horses in the stables, one that Baxter assured her was gentle, and yet she was still scared.

She had only been on the horse for a minute or so, though, and was trying to get the hang of how it felt to be on the animal, because it took some getting used to. But with Jake at her side she felt safe.

"Loosen your hold on the reins," Jake told her. "You're doing fine. You just need to relax a little."

"You'd better catch me if I fall off," Salina said.

"You know I will."

At his words, Salina loosened her grip. Nothing radical happened.

"Yes, that's good," Jake told her. "The horse isn't going to hurt you. It's safe. And it can also sense your fear. So you're better off just relaxing and going with the flow."

Salina took a deep breath and tried to do what Jake had suggested—relax. She wanted to enjoy the experience, and she wasn't sure she would if she couldn't let herself calm down. Sure, this animal was big, but so far it appeared quite gentle. She didn't have anything to worry about, did she?

When the horse began to suddenly move faster, Salina screamed. And then she giggled, feeling foolish. It wasn't as if the horse, named Charlie, had taken off in a full-out run. It simply began to trot.

"You clicked your heels against the horse's side," Jake explained. "That's why it began to trot."

"I did?"

"Yeah. As you were sitting up straight. But no reason to worry," Jake said as he jogged alongside her. "How does it feel to be on a horse?"

"It…" Salina took a deep breath and allowed herself to enjoy being on the horse. "It feels good."

Jake smiled at her and she smiled back at him. "Easy as pie," he told her.

Salina had to admit that he was right. "I'm on a horse!" she said happily. "I'm riding."

Glancing to her left, Salina looked at Riquet, who was on the other side of the large indoor arena. Baxter was guiding her around the arena, and her horse—larger than the one Salina had chosen—was trotting consistently. Riquet's smile was wide and luminescent. The experience for her was priceless.

"Riquet's making me look bad," Salina said good-naturedly. "Look at the way she's riding the horse so well. Hers is trotting happily along, not taking the baby steps mine is."

"You'll be an expert by the end of the day."

"I've never done this before," Salina said.

"You're doing great," Jake told her. "Don't worry."

"That's not what I mean. I'm trying to say that I've never done this before, so I wanted to thank you. Thank you for arranging this for me. Thank you for this experience."

"You're welcome." Jake grinned.

Lord, didn't he look like the most attractive man alive when he smiled.

"It's so beautiful here," Salina went on. "I have to admit, when you first suggested going horseback riding I was a little wary. I didn't know what to expect. I was certain we were going out in the snow, and I wasn't sure how much I would be able to handle in the cold. But in this covered dome it's so pleasant. And the picturesque beauty of this country area… thank you," she concluded.

The horse began to move a little faster, and instead of screaming Salina squealed this time, doing her best to hold in her fear. Within moments the horse was going at a steady trot, and Salina was enjoying every moment of it. Jake let her and the horse ride on their own for about ten seconds before he jogged to catch up with them. Reaching for the horse's reins, he took them from Salina and proceeded to guide the animal.

With Jake leading the horse, it walked and trotted around the arena for the next several minutes, and Salina found herself laughing as she reveled in this new experience.

When Jake brought the horse to a stop, Salina announced, "That was fun."

"You liked it?"

"I loved it."

"Then I guess we could come here more often," Jake said.

Salina looked at him again, staring at him with narrowed eyes. Was he trying to tell her that he wanted to build a relationship with her? She wanted to believe that, and so far today, she had reason to hope. But she was all too aware that, while one minute she got the feeling that he desired her, the next he was back to being Jake the Dad, Jake the widow. He was her employer and she was the nanny.

As if in answer to her question, Jake took her hand in his and squeezed it. Once again he held her gaze with those beautiful brown eyes of his.

Salina's heart began to race uncontrollably. There was something between them. She wasn't imagining it.

"Had enough?" Jake asked.

Of you touching me? Salina thought. *Never.* But she knew

what he meant, so she said, "Sure, I'm ready to come down now."

"All right. I'm going to get the horse to stop, and once it does, swing your right leg over to this side, so that both your legs are facing me. Then I'll help you down. You could keep one foot in the stirrup and come off on your own, but since you're not used to it, I'll help you."

"And you said you might not remember how to ride a horse." Salina smiled at Jake.

"I guess it's like riding a bike," he explained. "Ready?"

Salina did what he instructed her to do, bringing her right leg over to the other side of the horse and positioning her butt so that she could slide down the animal's side. Jake reached up and placed his hands on her hips and helped her down from the horse, and Salina got a little thrill at the touch of his hands on her body. She couldn't help remembering how his hands had roamed over every inch of her when she'd been naked.

And then he did something that totally surprised her. He gave her a quick peck on the lips.

Salina was too stunned to speak. She simply stared at him with wide eyes. Jake winked at her, letting her know that he had meant to kiss her. Then he quickly glanced across the arena at Riquet, and Salina understood that he had snuck in a kiss while his daughter wasn't looking.

A brief kiss, but it set her body on fire. How was it that Salina had so quickly developed strong feelings for this man?

"Daddy!"

As Riquet called out to Jake, he turned, breaking the mood between them. But Salina wasn't disappointed. She needed a bit of a breather, a moment to digest what had happened between her and Jake.

This Jake was different. The night they'd made love, he'd been hot with need and lust. There was no doubt that they

connected on a carnal level. But Salina had started to fear
that that was all their relationship was…a hot-and-bothered
one.

Today she was experiencing Jake the family man. Jake
the friend.

The friend who would also be her lover?

Because that's what Salina wanted. Friend and lover. The
entire package.

Salina heard a cell phone ring and wondered if it was
Jake's or Baxter's. A moment later she got her answer, when
she saw Jake lift his BlackBerry to his ear. He'd taken off
the Bluetooth earpiece that he'd been wearing in the car.

Salina watched as he walked to the bleachers in the indoor
arena and took a seat. She couldn't hear what he was saying,
but noted that his body language had changed.

A business call? Even on his day off he seemed to be connected to the office.

Minutes later Jake stood and stuffed his phone into the
inside of his jacket. He glanced in Riquet's direction. Baxter
was guiding her around on her horse. Riquet was chatting
happily, definitely in her element.

Jake made his way back over to Salina. She saw concern
in his eyes. "Is everything okay?"

"That was Maria," Jake explained.

Salina felt a spurt of panic. Was the woman coming back
already? Was her job with Riquet about to end?

"Her mother just died," Jake went on.

"Oh, no. That's awful."

Jake nodded solemnly. "That means she now has to help
with arranging the funeral, and I think she's keen on spending more time with her family. It's been a while since she's
been back home, and she probably feels a sense of guilt that
she wasn't there for her mother when she was still well."

"Of course."

"What that means for you, is that I would love for you to stay around a little bit longer to take care of Riquet. Will that be a problem?"

"How much longer will you need me?" Salina asked.

"I'm not sure yet. I told Maria to take all the time she needs. She's going to let me know."

This certainly wasn't what Salina had expected to hear, but by the same token, she hadn't been thinking beyond the next week—when she had expected that Maria would return to her job. That said, staying on in this job longer was going to put a bit of a kink in her long-term plans. Then again, she certainly hadn't heard about other employment opportunities yet, and she still needed to earn money. Without having money for culinary school, she wouldn't be able to see her dream come true.

No matter how much longer Jake needed her, she was in no position to tell him that she couldn't stay on.

But it wasn't the fact that she was in need of employment that was giving her pause. A part of her was excited that Jake needed her for more time. She didn't doubt they would end up making love again—and she wanted that. When he touched her all reason fled her mind. But in the days that he had been gone, and hardly speaking with her, insecurity had reared its ugly head. It made her realize that what she and Jake might have could only be a sexual relationship. And did she really want to stay on and continue working with him if that's all there was between them? The more she stayed with him—the more she engaged in hot kisses and hot passion—wasn't she only going to end up more brokenhearted in the end?

But the day she had spent with Jake so far was telling her that their attraction was more than simply sexual. She honestly believed that something was brewing between them.

One minute the idea of Maria returning had caused her

alarm, the next she was wondering if maybe it was best that her employment as a nanny ended.

Because the longer she continued to work for Jake, the more she would come to care for him. She knew that. Could feel that.

But what if he didn't reciprocate her feelings?

Her heart would be broken. And no amount of money could mend a broken heart.

That was what her rational brain told her as she looked at Jake. But her heart told her that she wasn't ready to walk away from him—no matter the emotional cost.

So she said, "Sure."

"Do you have any objections if the job was to last another six weeks, two months?"

"You think it will be that long before Maria returns?"

"I'm not saying that, I just wanted to ask you. Give you the chance to decide now." At the sound of Riquet's laughter, Jake gazed in that direction. Then he turned back to Salina. "I'm not sure what the future holds. I just want to know that you're ready for it," he concluded. "If it's going to be a problem, then I'm going to have to call an agency, see if another nanny—"

"That's not necessary," Salina told him. "You need me, you got me."

She felt an odd sensation as she finished her statement, realizing that for her, there was a double meaning to the comment, even if Jake didn't pick up on it.

"Good," he said. He smiled softly. "You've been good for Riquet. She seems happier than I've seen her in a good, long time. And that's saying a lot. I think you remind her of what she's been missing out on...her mother."

Salina drew in a soft intake of breath. To hear Jake say that touched her in the most profound way. It was a compliment of the highest order.

"I'm glad I've gotten along so well with her."

"I think she sees you as more of a mother figure than she does Maria. You're younger, more spontaneous. This whole idea of staying home and baking a cake for me for my birthday… I have to tell you, Maria wouldn't have it."

"Sometimes you have to break from the routine."

Jake's eyes crinkled as he looked at her. "Absolutely. And I love that you did that. The look on Riquet's face that day was priceless." Jake gestured toward his daughter, who was laughing happily. "You inspired me to break from my typical routine of staying home on a Saturday and working my butt off, and to do something that would create another memory for my daughter. Listen to her laugh… It's just the sweetest sound."

It was exactly that sort of thing that made Salina fall for Jake more and more. He had such a good heart. He had suffered a lot in his life and didn't deserve that. He deserved to be happy.

Salina had the overwhelming urge to reach out and touch him. He was hurting, she could still see a measure of sadness in his eyes. But it wasn't as intense as it had been before. She believed that he was starting to heal.

He deserved to heal. And Salina wanted to be the one who helped him to heal.

"You've been good for Riquet," Jake said as he looked into her eyes. "But you've also been good for me. You've been good for both of us."

Salina wanted to wrap her arms around his neck and kiss him. If his daughter wasn't in the room, she probably would have thrown caution to the wind and laid one on him.

But Jake took her hand in his, held it for a long moment. And that was as good as any kiss.

Maybe even better.

Chapter 14

At three o'clock, Jake, Salina and Riquet said their good-byes to Baxter and hit the road. Not only had Riquet gotten to ride a few horses, she'd also had a chance to visit Baxter's animals—the cows, pigs, chickens and goats. She'd taken a liking to one of the baby goats, and got a real kick out of hand-feeding the little animal.

Salina couldn't help noting that there was a marked change in Jake's demeanor. He looked happier and much more relaxed. It seemed that Riquet's own joy had rubbed off on him.

It did Salina's heart good to see both him and Riquet happy and enjoying themselves. By Jake's own admission, this kind of day of fun was something he had not enjoyed with his daughter in a very long time. Salina could only hope that the change in him would be a permanent one.

Shortly before they hit the road, Jake had received a call from his mother. From what Salina gathered, Bernice would be at his apartment, waiting for them when they got back. She wanted to take Riquet to her home in New Jersey for the duration of the weekend, bringing her back on Monday afternoon.

Salina had gotten the sense that Jake's mother hadn't taken to her the other day, and when they arrived back at the apartment that feeling was confirmed. Bernice's eyes widened ever so slightly when she saw Salina enter the apartment with Jake and Riquet. And the disapproval—while subtle—was clear to Salina.

"Hello, Mrs. McKnight," Salina said to Jake's mother, once Jake and Riquet had greeted her.

"Hello." The woman's voice was a little clipped.

"Grandma, we went to a farm and I got to ride three horses and feed a baby goat."

"Did you now?" Bernice said. She looked at Jake. "My, my, my, aren't you full of surprises these days?"

Jake didn't address his mother's comment. He simply said, "I'm surprised you're back in the city today. Twice in one week."

"I came in so I could enjoy a day of shopping with Joan. She's been feeling quite down since her husband died last year, and we haven't spent much time together since then. So when she called me this morning and asked if I was free to go shopping today, I jumped at the chance to get together with her. And I figured it would be nice to bring Riquet to Hoboken so she can see your father, since he didn't want to come in to the city to shop with me and Joan."

"No," Jake said with a little chuckle, "Dad's tolerance for shopping is pretty much nonexistent."

"Tell me about it. But he is looking forward to spending some time with his granddaughter, as am I." Bernice faced Riquet. "Are you excited about sleeping over at Grandma's house tonight?"

Riquet nodded energetically.

"I can prepare you something to eat," Salina suggested. She could whip up a dish with mushrooms and noodles fairly quickly.

"I've already eaten, but thank you. It's not a long drive to Hoboken, but I should probably hit the road with my granddaughter."

"That makes sense," Jake said.

"I can pack some clothes for Riquet," Salina offered.

"That's not necessary," Bernice said. "I can take care of gathering her belongings." She paused. "And since I'm here now, I guess my son will no longer need you for the evening. Really, Jake—did you have to take the nanny to the farm? I'm sure she had better things to do on a Saturday." Bernice smiled sweetly. "No, you can head off now. Enjoy a Saturday night with your friends."

Salina's pulse began to race. Was Jake's mother dismissing her? She looked at Jake, hoping that he would say that he wanted her to stay, because she wasn't ready to leave. But Jake didn't say anything. In fact, he avoided her eyes.

So they'd had a wonderful day, and now that was it? She was dismissed until Monday?

"I appreciate your dedication," Bernice said to Salina. "But don't be afraid to tell my son when he's pushing you too far. You can't be expected to spend your every waking hour working for him."

"My mother's right. I have been working you hard, Salina. You have definitely earned a day off."

Salina's stomach clenched. Jake wanted her to leave? After they had once again gotten close today, he was all but ushering her out the door?

And what was with that annoying business tone he put on every time his mother was here? Salina wanted to shake him. What about when he'd made love to her? He hadn't been all business *then*.

But Salina said nothing. If Jake was going to play Mr. Up-and-Down with his emotions, then fine. Salina may as well leave early. She hadn't spent much time with her sister since she began this job, so maybe they could do something together. Unless Emma had plans with her boyfriend, Zachary.

Salina got her coat, then walked over to Riquet. She bent down in front of the little girl. "Have a good time with your grandparents, okay?"

Riquet nodded. "I'll miss you." And then she threw her arms around Salina's neck.

It felt better than Salina would have imagined, to hold this little girl. She ended the hug more quickly than she would have liked. She didn't want to give the grandmother the sense that she was crossing some sort of professional line. Especially since Jake clearly wanted to keep up some sort of appearances around her.

Salina went to the door. "I'll see you both on Monday then," she said. "Goodbye, Mrs. McKnight."

"Goodbye," Jake's mother said, sounding definitely happier.

Salina opened the door and stepped into the hallway, completely baffled as to what had just happened. She was about to close the door behind her when she heard, "Hold on a second, Salina."

Jake. Her heart fluttered. Salina waited at the door for him to appear, tell her that he didn't want her to leave.

He got to the door and stepped into the hallway, pulling the door mostly closed behind him. "Don't go far," he said in a hushed tone.

Salina looked up at him in confusion. "Pardon me?"

"I don't really want you to leave. But I think it will be

better for my mother to head out with Riquet before you return."

Salina narrowed her eyes. "You don't want your mother to know that you want me to stay?"

"It's complicated. But yeah, it's better this way." He paused. "Will you wait? Maybe go do a little bit of shopping until I call you?"

Salina's jaw tightened. She wanted to tell him that no, if he couldn't tell his mother that he wanted her to stay, then she would go. Jake was a grown man, one who didn't need his mother's approval to date someone.

But Salina had to concede that Bernice didn't really like her, and maybe she was the kind of meddling mother who would give her son a hard time. She had to respect Jake's reasons. He knew his mother, after all.

Still, Salina didn't like this.

"Please," Jake said.

"I guess I can hang around for a bit," Salina said noncommittally. "But if it takes too long for you to call, I'm gonna be gone."

"Fair enough."

Then Salina turned and walked down the hallway.

In the wake of Salina's departure, Jake felt odd. His stomach was slightly unsettled, as though he had just eaten something that didn't agree with him. He supposed he felt bad about the way she had left so abruptly—especially when it hadn't been his desire to have her leave at that moment, but his mother's.

Worse, he felt like a teenager sneaking in some time to talk to her at the door, tell her that his desire was for her to really stay. He was a thirty-five-year-old man, and the look on her face had said that she couldn't understand why he was trying to secretly ask her to stay, instead of letting his mother know of his true desire.

The problem was, Salina didn't know his mother. Didn't know how she liked to involve herself in his private affairs. She had already made her opinion clear—she didn't want him getting involved with Salina, emotionally or otherwise. It wasn't that Jake was about to obey his mother, he just didn't need the headache. And before he knew explicitly what was happening between him and Salina, why bother to involve his mother?

Jake was in the living room with Riquet when his mother exited the child's room with a small suitcase. She had packed the few clothes that his daughter would need for her two-night trip.

"Jake, will you come here for a moment?"

Jake rose from the sofa and followed his mother into his kitchen. Facing him, she said, "Anything you want to tell me about your relationship with your nanny?"

"Like what?"

His mother gave him a knowing look. "I never knew you to take Maria horseback riding or skating at Rockefeller Center."

"And that's exactly why Salina has been so good for Riquet," Jake said. "She's younger, more spontaneous. She brings a different vibe. Riquet has really enjoyed having her here."

"Only Riquet?" His mother raised an eyebrow.

"Mom…"

"Please don't do anything foolish," she advised him. "Have you called Elizabeth yet?"

"No I haven't, and I don't plan to."

"Jake. Please just think about it. Think about everything I said. You're getting to the point where you're going to have to get involved in city politics if you plan to have a political career. With a woman like Elizabeth by your side—"

"Mom, please," Jake said firmly. "I don't want to have this conversation again."

Bernice stared at him for a long moment, then sighed softly. If she wanted to say something else, she thought better of it.

"You and Riquet ought to hit the road," Jake said.

Bernice stepped toward him and gave him a kiss on the cheek, and then a hug. "I love you, son," she said. "You know I just want what's best for you."

"I know."

She eased back and smiled at him. "All right, then. I'll get going with Riquet. Don't work too hard. I'll bring Riquet back on Monday in the afternoon. She can miss a day of preschool. She doesn't see us all that often."

Spontaneity. It made Jake think of Salina. "Sounds good."

Jake saw his mother out and gave Riquet a huge hug as they said goodbye. She was smiling brightly, excited about her sleepover trip. He looked at his daughter with fondness, thinking about how well she had fared in the wake of her mother's death. She was still a bright and happy child, with love to give in leaps and bounds.

After Riquet and his mother left, Jake went to the phone and dialed Salina's number. The phone rang three times, and he thought she wasn't going to answer it—that perhaps she was too upset with him and had decided she was heading home to Brooklyn, after all.

But she picked up before the phone rang a fourth time. She said without preamble, "Is your mother gone?"

"Yes," Jake said, sighing softly. He knew how juvenile he sounded, trying to sneak her in after his mother was gone. But for now, he wanted to keep his relationship with Salina private. "Do you want to come back—or would you rather head home?"

There was a long pause, and Jake wondered if Salina was still on the line. "Salina—?"

"I'm on my way."

"Jake," Salina began, when she was back in the apartment sitting on the sofa with him, "what's the deal with your mother?"

"My relationship with my mother is complicated. I knew she would give me an earful if she realized that I wanted you to stay. I haven't dated anyone since Janine. And if my mother thought I was getting romantically involved with you… Well, let's just say she would think it was very inappropriate for me to be involved with someone who is working for me." Jake paused. "Remember, I told you about her aspirations for my political career?"

"Yes," Salina said, nodding.

"Well, my getting involved with you is exactly the kind of thing that my mother would say would tarnish my image. You're my nanny, yada yada yada." Pausing, Jake slid closer to her on the sofa and slipped his arm around her. "Please don't be offended. I simply don't want to complicate the matter, where my mother is concerned."

Salina nodded. She couldn't blame Jake for wanting to be cautious about their relationship and his mother's reaction to it. The truth was, if *they* didn't know what their relationship was, how was Jake supposed to explain it to anyone else? And she could understand that his mother would have a lot of questions.

"I wanted to have a guilt-free night with you—the kind I couldn't have if my mother gave me a lecture about all the reasons I shouldn't be involved with you."

"You don't owe me an explanation," Salina said.

Jake frowned slightly, as if he sensed she wasn't entirely happy with him. He took her hand in his and said, "I have a surprise for you."

"You do?"

Jake nodded. "Yeah. It's a gift, really. It's part of the reason I wanted you back here. Among other things…."

Now Salina started to feel excitement. "You bought me a gift?"

"It's in my bedroom. I wanted to give it to you last night, but you didn't seem like you were in the best mood. Not that I blame you—I know I've been up and down. I haven't dated in so long, Salina, I feel like I don't know how to do it anymore. You just have to bear with me. Okay?"

Salina nodded. "Okay."

"I got the gift for you when I was at the charity auction. Well, I didn't know if I would get it for sure, but I put a high enough bid on it that I would hopefully be the one to snag it."

"You're killing me here," Salina said, a laugh in her voice. "I'm dying to know what you got me."

"Let me get it," Jake said. "Or you can follow me to the bedroom, if you like…."

Salina was as giddy as a child on Christmas morning as she jumped up from the sofa and followed Jake to his bedroom.

Jake had bought something for her? And on the night of the charity fundraiser? No wonder he had come back to the apartment wanting to make love to her…

All week he hadn't said anything. And here Salina had come to believe that he had been able to put her out of his mind while he'd been away, without a second thought.

Now she was seeing things in a whole different light.

"I saw this and thought of you right away," Jake explained

as he opened the door and entered the bedroom. "I hope you like it."

Salina had hoped that her anticipation would end once Jake opened the bedroom door, but instead the surprise continued. On his desk was a massive, gift-wrapped box in elegant gold foil, topped off with a white satin bow.

"Jake...?"

"Open it."

Squealing happily, Salina ran toward the desk and began ripping the wrapping paper off the present. As the packaging came into view, Jake said, "I hear it's the best of the best. All-clad, copper-core— I don't really know what that means, and maybe you've already got a fabulous cookware set—"

"Oh, my goodness, a cookware set!" Salina exclaimed. It touched her to know that Jake had bought something for her that related to her dream. It meant he cared. Salina continued to tear off the gold foil paper. "No, I don't have one like this."

"You like it?"

"Like it?" she asked as she hurriedly dropped the wrapping paper onto the floor. "I love—"

But her words died in her throat when she saw the name on the package. The scrawled celebrity signature.

A few moments passed, then Jake asked, "What's the matter? It's the wrong kind? I figured, if Donald Martin endorsed it, it had to be a great one."

Salina suddenly found it hard to breathe. She glanced at Jake, saw the concern in his eyes. "It's not that it's the wrong kind... It's—"

Jake placed his hands on her shoulders. "What is it? What's wrong?"

Salina stepped back from the box and turned away. It was a lovely gift. But it was a Donald Martin cookware set. She couldn't ever use this without remembering what had happened.

"Salina?" Jake's voice was laced with worry.

"I appreciate you buying me something, but I can't accept this."

"Why not?"

"Because it's from Donald Martin. And I want nothing that ever reminds me of that man."

Chapter 15

Jake's gut clenched. Seeing the distress on Salina's face, in her body language, he realized that something horrible had happened between her and Donald Martin. "What did he do to you?"

Salina didn't speak right away. Jake stepped toward her and placed his finger beneath her chin, forcing her to meet his gaze. "Tell me."

"I worked for him. I thought that when I met him, my dream of becoming a chef was certain to become a reality. He offered me the chance to work at his restaurant, with the promise that I would likely head up a new location he was planning to open in the next year or so. I should have known better. I should have known it was too good to be true."

"What did he do to you?" Jake asked through gritted teeth. If Donald Martin had hurt her...

Salina exhaled harshly. "I don't like to think about it."

"If he hurt you in some—"

"I thought he was offering me the opportunity of a lifetime. I was excited about working for him. He was very hard on me in the beginning, and then did a total one-eighty. He became a little flirtatious. But since he was married, I didn't take him too seriously, and he never crossed a line. Until…"

Jake glanced at her. "Until when?"

"Until the night he had me head to a condo on the Upper East Side, where we would be catering a private dinner. Only, when I got there the only person there was Donald, and he had this whole, elaborate, romantic dinner set up—for me and him."

Jake clenched his fists. He couldn't remember the last time he had felt this kind of rage. He had the overwhelming desire to seek out Donald Martin and teach the man a lesson he wouldn't soon forget.

But more than that, he wanted to pull Salina into his arms and comfort her. Let her know that he would protect her from the Donald Martins of the world, keep her safe.

"Did he violate you?"

"I fought him off."

"Tell me he didn't hurt you." Jake needed to hear that Salina had been okay. Because if not, Donald would need to pay for what he'd done.

"He didn't get to. I fought him off and ran out of there."

Jake gathered her into his arms and wrapped her in an embrace. "I couldn't believe what was happening," she went on. "And when he first came on to me, I asked him what he was doing, pointed out that he was married. But he was a man with a plan. He wanted me in his bed. I think he is used to getting his way all the time because he has money, and he didn't believe I would have the audacity to reject him. When I had to run out of his penthouse suite, it became clear to me that I couldn't keep working for him. But to add insult to injury, Donald sent me a text afterward saying that I was fired."

Jake's heart was beating erratically, he was that upset. All that mattered to him right now was offering Salina comfort and protection. "I'm sorry you had to go through that."

Salina leaned her head against his shoulder. "It just proved that if something seems too good to be true, it is. Here I thought I'd found this amazing shortcut to success, and it was all a lie."

Jake eased back and looked at her. He was impressed by her demeanor. She had a fighting spirit, and clearly had been able to take care of herself quite well. Even in her retelling of the story, she didn't seem as though she was about to fall apart.

"You know your firing was unlawful, and you could—"

"I know. My sister gave me an earful about what I should do, how I could get justice legally—but I just wanted to let the matter go and move on. And that, in a nutshell, is how I came to work for you."

Jake stroked her cheek softly. "Well, I guess in some way I could thank him then. Though I could also wring his neck."

Salina grinned up at him. "Now that's something I wouldn't mind seeing." She chuckled softly. "Not really—don't get any ideas. But I love that you care."

"I do care," Jake said softly. He gave her a soft peck on the lips. "I do..."

And then he moved his mouth to her ear and whispered hotly, "Let me show you how much."

As Jake lowered his face to meet hers, Salina raised her face to meet his. And then their lips came together in an explosion of passion. This kiss was nothing like the soft peck they'd shared at Baxter's farm. This one was a fireball erupting from a volcano.

The intensity was beyond anything Salina had imagined possible. She opened her own mouth wide, giving Jake more access. He delved his tongue deep into the moist recesses of her welcoming mouth, and the sensations—oh, goodness, the sensations—it was incredible.

Closing her eyes, Salina slipped her arms around Jake's neck. She sighed happily as his tongue twisted with hers.

He gripped her tightly, pressing his broad hands against her back. She opened her mouth wider still, needing to taste more of him.

The kiss deepened and became more urgent, the only sound filling the room their heavy breathing. Salina ran her hands across Jake's wide shoulders, loving the feel of his strong muscles. Jake's hands moved up and down her back before going lower and settling on her behind. He pulled her body against him with force, and Salina could feel the hard evidence of his desire for her.

Heat consumed her from head to toe. Never in her life had she ever felt this kind of all-consuming passion for a man. She didn't care if there wasn't a tomorrow with Jake. All she wanted was right now.

She *needed* right now. No matter what came next, she wanted tonight.

And that wasn't like her. She wasn't the type to jump recklessly into a relationship when she wasn't even sure if the man she wanted was capable of giving her his heart.

She was the first one to reach her hand down toward the hem of Jake's shirt. Then she slipped her fingertips beneath the fabric and felt his warm skin. A satisfied moan escaped her lips.

He felt amazing. His skin was smooth, his muscles hard, and Salina couldn't get enough of touching him. She let her fingers explore, teasing his skin with the tips of each digit. She stroked them back and forth over his body until he groaned in satisfaction.

Salina never knew that any kind of sound Jake emitted could give her a surge of power, but his groan did. She pressed her fingertips into his flesh, somehow holding back from dragging her nails against his skin—which was what she really wanted to do. That's how strong her need for him was.

Jake raised his hands from her butt to the hem of her shirt. And oh, that first touch of fingers against her skin was heaven. He trailed his fingers upward, caressing her skin with reverence. And when he got to her bra his hands stopped.

Salina's breath caught in her throat. When they had first made love, it had been frenzied and fueled by need, but tonight was different. There was tenderness in Jake's touch.

She wanted to get naked with him again. She wanted to feel his body against hers, skin-to-skin, the way it was intended for man and woman to be. And this time she wanted to be able to savor it all night long.

Jake let his fingers linger on the back of her bra, teasing her by stroking his fingers across the length of the strap.

Easing his head back, he gazed down at her. And then he loosened the bra's fastenings.

His fingers skimmed her skin as his eyes held hers. Yes, this was different than the night he had returned from the charity event. Something about the way he was taking his time with her tonight made it feel as though they were about to make love for the first time.

"Jake, you have no idea how you're making me feel."

She leaned into him and kissed him more deeply, silently urging him to continue taking her clothes off. Jake moved his hands from her back in synchronicity, bringing both of his palms to the sides of her breasts at the same time. He stroked her flesh, driving her crazy with anticipation. Her nipples were already erect, desire flowing through her like an electric current.

Finally, Jake's hands moved to Salina's taut peaks. He tweaked the tips of her nipples and the pleasurable sensations were beyond anything Salina could have imagined. Not even with her most serious boyfriend in the past did this kind of contact feel so utterly amazing.

She wanted more of him. Reaching her own hands farther up the front of his shirt, she stroked his flat nipples. She let her hands wander over his strong pecs. He was a chocolate Adonis, and Salina wanted to taste him.

Jake kissed her again, slow and sweet. She broke the kiss and eased backward, sighing softly when Jake's hands fell from her breasts. Then she gripped his shirt in her fists and pulled it over his head. When it was free from his body, she tossed it to the floor.

Jake did the same to her, taking off her shirt first, and then her bra. He flung both pieces of clothing onto the floor next to his discarded shirt.

Once again he looked at her. First into her eyes, with an expression that spoke volumes of meaning. What Salina read in this gaze was that what they were about to do was not simply have sex, but make love.

The first time, they'd had sex. Tonight was about more.

Jake's gaze lowered, creating a path of heat along Salina's skin. His eyes took in her breasts and a small breath of air escaped his lips.

"You're lovely," he said. "Absolutely perfect."

The words were like an aphrodisiac, turning Salina on even more. She leaned forward, once again pressing her lips against Jake's. This time when they kissed, it was slow and passionate and simmering with a sweet kind of heat. He gently framed her face, and Salina loved the way that felt, him holding her face as he kissed her, stroking his fingers along her jaw. Goodness, it was magnificent.

Jake's lips moved from her mouth to her cheek, and then

to the underside of her jaw. He let his lips and tongue linger there, eliciting moans of pleasure from her, before moving to the next patch of her skin. He kissed a trail to the front of her neck, and then farther down to the area between her breasts. Salina found herself holding her breath as he inched his way toward her peaks of pleasure.

"The first night, I rushed this," Jake said in a low voice. "Tonight I want to do it right."

Still, he didn't touch her nipples. Instead, gently placing his hands on her ribs, he guided her backward onto the bed. When she was on her back he trailed his hands up the sides of her torso, while his mouth rained kisses between the area of her breasts. Then he moved his hands along the side her breasts, stroking her fullness while his mouth moved toward one peak. Salina watched him, amazed at the way he treated her body with such reverence. He looked at her and touched her with the kind of gentleness combined with passion that said she was an exquisite piece of art, not just the object of his lust.

And then his mouth came down on her nipple and Salina stopped thinking altogether. Nothing had felt as good as this. She arched her back and gripped the sheets, wave after wave of bliss taking her to a height she hadn't been to before. Her body was overloaded with glorious sensations.

All too soon Jake pulled back, and Salina sighed softly in protest. But he was now hovering over her, and he placed his fingers beneath the waistband of her panties. Again Salina found herself holding her breath. Jake then slowly pulled her pants and underwear off her body and tossed them to the side. He kissed the inside of one of her legs, moving higher, inch by inch, until he reached the center of her thighs. He gazed at her, drank in the sight of her womanhood, and Salina felt empowered rather than awkward.

The way he looked at her—had anything been more potent?

"You are so incredibly beautiful," Jake told her.

As he stroked her, bringing out more heated sensations in her body, Salina moaned, enjoying every delicious thrill his touch elicited. And when he lowered his mouth onto her most sensitive spot she gasped. The pleasure was so intense. Perhaps too intense. She held her breath and tried to calm her body so she could relax and enjoy every amazing moment.

Jake was a gentle and skilled lover. His tongue made her delirious, bringing her to the edge. She gripped the bed sheets and moaned his name as he skillfully pleased her until she could take no more. Her body gave in to a blissful climax, and she cried out his name as she rode the wave of pleasure.

"Jake—oh, my God. Oh, sweetheart…"

Jake eased back and kissed her inner thigh. Salina was in heaven. There was no doubt about it. She never wanted to leave this place she had found with Jake, this place of magic.

"Do you want me to continue?" he asked.

"If you stop now, I'll never forgive you!" Salina was shocked by her own exuberant reply, but she knew there was no way she could stop now. She'd had a taste of him, but it was only an appetizer. She was ready for the full three-course meal.

"This isn't like the first time we were together," he told her. "That first time my need for you consumed me, and I didn't take the time I should have with you. Tonight, if you want me to touch and kiss that sweet body of yours all night long and refrain from satisfying myself, I'll do that."

"I want us to satisfy each other," Salina said. She appreciated his respect for her, that he was concerned that he had failed in some way as a lover the first time, especially at a moment like this, when his own desire had to be bubbling forward.

It made her care for him all the more.

"Take off all your clothes," Salina whispered into his ear.

Her body still feeling the thrill of his touch, she watched Jake stand and remove his pants and briefs. She reveled in the sight of his naked body. He let her look her fill before he went to his night table and took a condom from the drawer.

When he had the condom on, Salina sat up and said, "Come here." She reached for him, slipping her arms around his back and pulling him down onto her. They kissed, hot and sweet at the same time.

She parted her thighs and Jake gingerly settled his body on top of hers. She kissed his chin and then his neck, waiting for that sweet moment when their bodies would unite.

And then he entered her, carefully, slowly, and the feeling was so exquisite that Salina closed her eyes and simply savored it, hoping to commit it to memory.

She was in love with him. That was the thought that came into Salina's mind. It wasn't simply because of her reaction to this touch, her reaction to them being together. It was him. Even the way he touched her with such gentle reverence showed her just how much of a good man he was. And for Salina, he was irresistible.

She wanted to tell him that she was in love with him, and yet she didn't. Those were serious words, words that could scare him off. So she would say nothing for now, and hope that in the morning he didn't regret being with her. Rather, she hoped he would see that they could have a wonderful future together.

But once Jake eased his head down to her breast and suckled her nipple as he was making love to her, all thoughts fled Salina's mind. She savored the feelings overpowering her—both the blissful sensations, as well as the feeling of love filling her heart.

Chapter 16

The next morning Salina awoke in Jake's arms. She smiled as she remembered where she was and how the night had played out. She was resting her head against his chest, and his arm was draped around her waist.

She felt happy and safe and content.

And loved.

Raising her head, she peered at Jake. His eyes were closed, and the steady rise and fall of his chest told her that he was still asleep.

Carefully, Salina extricated herself from his arms. She needed to use the bathroom and didn't want to wake him as she crawled out of bed.

There was only one other door in the room beside the one that led to the apartment at large, and Salina figured that had to lead to his en suite bathroom. She opened it. Inside, she saw a narrow hallway that led to a large bathroom area. On one side of the hallway were open doors, beyond which were clothes neatly arranged on hangers. Men's clothes that obviously belonged to Jake. On the opposite side was a door that Salina guessed housed another closet.

Salina used the bathroom, and on her way out her curiosity got the better of her. She opened the doors opposite Jake's closet to see what was inside.

She expected to find more male clothing, or perhaps an empty space. But what she saw shocked her. Dresses and shoes filled the area. Expensive-looking gowns and cocktail dresses, as well as rows of designer shoes.

Janine's clothes? After all this time, Jake still had her clothes in the closet, as if she might return home at any moment.

"Hey."

At the sound of Jake's voice, Salina jumped backward from the closet doors in fright. Then she turned and looked at him. "I'm sorry," she began quickly, feeling too guilty to even enjoy the sight of him naked. "I shouldn't have—"

"It's okay," Jake told her.

Salina felt awkward, but Jake said nothing else, just went past her into the bathroom. She returned to his king-size bed and slipped her naked body back under the covers.

Less than two minutes later Jake joined her. He pulled her into his arms and she once again rested her head on his chest.

"I bet you're wondering why I still have her clothes," he said softly.

Salina didn't want to lie, so she said nothing.

"I don't know. I guess…I guess I didn't have the heart to get rid of them." He paused. "Some days it's still so hard to wrap my head around. One minute Janine was here as a living, breathing, vibrant person. How could she be gone in an instant?"

Salina felt a spurt of jealousy, but told herself she was

being not only ridiculous but insensitive. How crazy was it to be jealous of a dead woman?

"I can only imagine how hard that was for you," she said.

Jake strummed his fingers along her lower back. "Yeah."

"Was it a collision with another car?" Salina asked, broaching the subject gently. "A drunk driver?"

"No. It was a one-car collision. Janine's car careened off the road once she crossed the bridge into New Jersey."

Jake fell silent and Salina did, too. She listened to the sound of his heavy breathing, not sure what to say. Losing a loved one was devastating, and no matter how other people said they understood, you couldn't really, unless you'd experienced it. Salina didn't want to say anything that Jake might deem as thoughtless. Rather, she preferred to lend an ear if he wanted to talk.

"You know what's always bothered me?" Jake said suddenly. "Janine was supposed to be heading to see her parents. At least that's what she said to me before she left. But her parents are in Albany, and she was heading in the wrong direction. If she was heading to Albany, what was she doing driving into New Jersey?"

Salina eased up and looked at him. "Did she have friends in New Jersey? Other family?"

"My parents," Jake said. "But they said they hadn't expected her." He let out a weary sigh. "I got the sense she was unhappy with me for some reason. That she was making an excuse to head out of the apartment. Maybe she simply wanted to go for a drive...I don't know. But something about how she left that night has never sat right with me.

"I never knew my wife to lie to me, and I don't think for a minute that she was off meeting another man. That's not what I'm saying." Jake paused and Salina nodded her understanding. "It's more that I felt a general sense of unease before she left."

Salina was silent for a long while. Then, in a gentle voice, she asked, "Are you sure what you're feeling isn't a sense of guilt? You know…that maybe if you'd said something or done something she wouldn't have left and she wouldn't have died?"

"I know what you mean," Jake said, "and I've asked myself that time and again. But the odd feeling wasn't something I manufactured after she died. I felt it before she left the apartment. When the devastating news came—and given the location where she'd crashed—I tried to replay in my mind everything that had happened that evening. All I could think was that she'd been unhappy with me about something. Maybe I'd said something to upset her, done something she was mad at me for but hadn't said. Maybe she was angry because I'd been working too much or I failed to notice a new hairstyle. Something innocuous, but something that mattered to her. Did she leave the apartment upset…and was it because of me?"

Salina's heart spasmed. Because she heard the unspoken thought that she knew had to come next: *Am I the reason my wife died?*

Easing her body upward, she kissed Jake on the cheek. "You can't blame yourself. You know that, right? It was just an accident. No one's fault."

"I just wonder…"

"Jake, don't. Don't do this to yourself. You're not the reason your wife died."

Jake tightened his grip on her. "I know…"

"You know it but you don't feel it," Salina supplied. Because she could see in his eyes that he carried guilt.

"In the beginning, the thinking and wondering about it drove me crazy. The not knowing. That's why I had to throw myself into work. To forget…"

Salina couldn't help asking, "If you want to forget, why do you have all her clothes in the closet?"

"So I always remember what I lost." Jake paused, and Salina thought he was about to say something else. After a long moment he went on, "I never planned to date anyone ever again. I planned for it to be me and Riquet forever." He met her eyes now, held them. "You're the first woman I've been with. Somehow you broke through my walls. What I've shared with you is something I don't take lightly. I just want you to know that."

"I do." Salina gave Jake a soft kiss on the lips. "I do."

She gave him another kiss, and this one grew deeper. Jake pulled her naked body onto his. As they kissed tenderly and with meaning, Salina felt Jake becoming aroused, just as she was.

And when they made love again, Salina knew that she had found heaven on earth.

As much as she didn't want to, Salina left Jake's apartment in the afternoon—after they'd spent the entire morning naked and in bed, capped off by a late breakfast of omelets with cheese and mushrooms. Jake needed to get some work done, and Salina was looking forward to spending some time with her sister.

She was floating on cloud nine as she left Jake's place, knowing that people must have been wondering about the silly smirk on her face as she rode the train back to Brooklyn. Jake had offered to drive her to Brooklyn since Ed was off for the weekend, but Salina had declined. She knew he hadn't done any work thus far this weekend, not with the trip to the farm and with the night and morning they'd shared, so she had acted like a mature adult and had torn herself away from him and found her own way home.

But she couldn't stop thinking of him every waking moment on the way back to her sister's place.

Salina was all set to sit down and tell her sister all that had transpired—until she entered the apartment and saw Emma curled up on one corner of the sofa, crying her eyes out.

"Emma? My God, what's wrong?"

Emma looked up at Salina with tear-stained cheeks. "It's over," she sobbed. "It's over between me and Zachary."

"What?" Salina asked. She went to the sofa and sat beside her sister. "I thought you two were very happy."

"So did I. But apparently Zachary's brother is getting married to some homemaker whose only goal is to be home with the kids that they're going to have. And suddenly I'm not a good enough woman for him anymore."

"Nooo."

Emma dabbed at her cheeks with a tissue. "Don't get me wrong—I respect a woman's right to work at home if she so chooses. But Zachary has known me for years. He has known that my goal has always been to become a partner at my law firm. Now he's telling me I'm too busy for him, that it's clear I'm not devoted to *him.* Apparently, I'm no longer good wife material."

Salina gasped. "He did *not* say that."

"Oh, yes he did. I was stunned. He has always supported my goal—or so I thought. And it's not like I just became a lawyer last week. I was a lawyer when he met me. Plus, I've been absorbed in this big case for months—I know that's taking away from the time I could be spending with him. But he either has to love me for who I am or not at all." Emma paused. "I guess he went for the not at all option."

At those words, Emma choked up and began to cry again. Salina put her arms around her. "I'm so sorry. I know this hurts, Emma. I'm really, really sorry. But let's face it—it's *his* loss. You know that, right?"

Emma brushed her tears away almost angrily as she looked at Salina. Now the lawyer-fighter was back in her eyes. "Oh, yes. I know that. It just…it just sucks for right now. But I know one day I will meet the man of my dreams, someone who's going to love me for me, accept me for who I am and not be threatened by my career."

At the talk of finding the right man, Salina couldn't help thinking about Jake. After last night, she was certain she had found the man of her dreams. But did Jake feel the same way about her?

Their growing relationship had definitely been up and down, and while it was up right now, Salina knew that it would be foolish to totally let her guard down. In fact, her sister's despair was driving that point home. In Jake's case, he might be totally interested in her, but Salina knew that his late wife still had to be in his heart, at least to a degree.

It was possible that he simply would never get over his late wife. It wasn't as though he and Janine had had problems that turned ugly between them. She had died—and at the time of her death Jake had clearly adored her. She'd been on a pedestal in his eyes, from everything Salina could tell.

But two years was a long time to mourn someone. Not that Salina would ever make light of his loss. She knew it had to be absolutely devastating. But he deserved to have love in his life, and not just throw himself into work. And she hated to think that guilt over Janine's death might prevent him from finding love with someone else.

And if Janine had been his first love, it could possibly be a greater challenge….

Sometimes it was hard to get past heartbreak and truly make yourself available for another relationship. Her friend Brianne had done it. But Salina knew that there was a part of Emma that likely still burned a torch for Sean—the one who got away when she was in college.

Would Jake always burn a torch for his late wife?

"I'm sorry," Emma said. She patted Salina's hand. "It looks like I've put you in a down mood."

"No," Salina said. Though she wasn't being totally honest. She was suddenly back to feeling insecure about her relationship with Jake. "I'm okay."

"I've hardly seen you. Jake must be working you really hard."

"Um, yeah." An image of last night—of her and Jake naked together in his bed—popped into her mind.

"I told you Jake is a workaholic."

Salina nodded, not saying anything. He certainly had been a workaholic in the bedroom last night...

"Salina?" Emma asked, one of her eyebrows shooting up.

"Hmm?"

Now Emma pursed her lips as she stared at her. "What's going on, sis?"

"Who says anything's going on?"

"Look at the way your right eye is narrowing. That always happens when you're not being truthful..."

"It is not," Salina protested.

"Oh, my gosh—it just happened again!" Emma stared at her the way she might stare at someone on the stand in a courtroom, trying to break them. Then she gasped, as she obviously came to her own conclusion as to what was going on. "Are you...*is there something going on between you and Jake?*"

Salina sucked in a deep breath. She had to tell her sister. She had to tell someone about how close she and Jake had gotten. "I think...I think I'm falling for him."

"Oh, my God. *What?*"

"I know it's fast, and that's why I didn't want to say anything. Part of me feels that what's happening is a dream. But he's just so extraordinary. I don't know...we just click."

"You slept with Jake," Emma said. Not a question.

"I...I know it wasn't the smartest thing. It just—well, it just happened."

Emma's eyes brightened. "Jake, the workaholic...and my sister. Huh."

"I don't even know what's happening between us," Salina said, her first inclination being to justify what they'd done, downplay it. Then, remembering how wonderful the evening had been with Jake, she beamed. "But I have to say, I've never felt this amazing before. *Ever.*"

Emma, who minutes ago had been glum, smiled from ear-to-ear. "I can't believe someone got through Jake's wall. He's a great guy. He deserves to be happy. Most of us at the firm wondered if he would ever date again."

Salina's heart filled with warmth. It was nice to know that she was the one who had been able to break through his emotional wall.

"You're really happy for me?" Salina asked. "You don't think I'm foolish for falling for him so quickly?"

"I've been dating Zachary for over two years. And out of the blue, he dumps me because he suddenly realizes I'm not The One." Emma halted. Swallowed visibly. "Who's to say it should take months and months to fall in love? The truth is, the first time I ever fell in love I know that it happened the very first night."

"Sean," Salina said softly. "Have you ever tried to find—"

"That's ancient history, sis."

Emma smiled, but it didn't reach her eyes. And Salina realized in that instant that her sister *did* still carry a torch for her old flame.

But she also knew there was no point in broaching that subject with Emma. She would shut Salina down in an instant.

So she spoke about Jake. "I really like him," Salina said.

"And I just adore Riquet." Pausing, she sighed softly. "I feel this incredible high when I'm with Jake…but he's been a little hot and cold. Mostly hot lately," she added with a sheepish grin. "But I worry that he might not truly have his heart to give. I know Janine meant a lot to him."

"I can't say she didn't," Emma said, her tone gentle. "But he has to move on at some point. Why not with you?"

Why not indeed? That was the thought that Salina clung to. And with the memory of how hot and emotional she and Jake had been between the sheets the night before, it wasn't hard.

Chapter 17

Over the next few days, Salina had only reasons of hope concerning her relationship with Jake. He was a different person. While still busy with work, he hadn't erected the wall again. And though he was conscious of not displaying any questionable affection toward Salina in front of Riquet, he sneaked in kisses here and there, and generally made her feel secure in the fact that his desire for her was real.

On Wednesday evening, after Riquet was in bed, Jake sat beside Salina in the living room. Salina was enjoying the way she and Jake were stealing time to flirt and kiss, while not jumping into bed. She knew that Jake wanted to take more precautions because of his daughter, and the buildup of sexual tension would only make the next time they made love be that much sweeter.

Jake sat beside Salina and took her hand in his. "I was wondering if you would like to go to an event with me," he said.

"An event? What kind of event?"

"It's a heritage celebration for Black History Month, put on by the Congressional Black Caucus. There'll be dinner, an awards ceremony. The event itself is a fundraiser for the CBC's virtual library project."

"Wow. Sounds…important."

"It's a pretty big event," Jake said. Then, "You remember I told you that my father was in politics, that I've also considered entering the political arena? Well, there will be African-American congressional members in attendance, as well. When it comes to politics and political aspirations, it's always good to get out and be seen. But the fundraiser itself is a good cause, and it's an entertaining evening."

"Congressional members…that sounds like an event that would happen in DC."

"Didn't I mention that?" Jake asked. "It's in DC."

Salina's eyes widened. "You want me to go to an event with you in Washington, DC?"

Jake nodded. "Friday night."

"Friday? That's two days from now."

"I know. And I wasn't sure I was going to go. Now, I figure…well, it might be a good time for us to sneak in some private time." Leaning forward, Jake kissed her cheek.

Oh, how the kiss felt good. "B-but what about Riquet? DC is what—four hours away?"

Jake stroked her cheek. "Not if you take a plane."

"And if it's an evening event, that'll mean spending the night—"

Jake gently grazed her earlobe with his teeth. "Exactly."

Salina drew in a sharp breath of air. "You want me to go to DC with you, to some big event, and spend the night there with you?"

"Why are you so surprised?"

This was a big step. Wasn't it? Yes, they were sexually

involved, and emotionally, as well. But an event like this—this was big.

"But what about Riquet?" Salina repeated.

Jake chuckled softly. "I have a babysitter I call for occasions like this. A day here, a night there. Janine and I used to use her on occasion when we went out of town, or just wanted a grown-up night to ourselves."

Janine… One way or another, she always came up. On one hand, it was to be expected. Janine had been Jake's wife. The mother of his child. But on the other hand, Salina worried that the memory of his late wife might always hang over them like a cloud.

"Are you saying you want some grown-up time with me?" Salina asked, raising a suggestive eyebrow.

"Hell, yes. I most definitely do." Jake winked at her, then pulled her into his arms. "Especially after the fantastic time we had this past weekend. It's been killing me that I can't touch you this week…but we decided it was better this way. I want another long and uninterrupted night with you. Did I say 'long'?" Jake grinned devilishly. "Do you have a problem with that?"

"No." Salina was aware that her answer lacked resolve.

"You don't seem so sure," Jake said.

A beat passed. "To tell the truth, I *am* a bit unsure."

"Why?"

"It's just… I've never been to some fancy political event before. I won't know what to say, what to do."

"You'll be fine," Jake told her. He nuzzled his nose against her neck. "I'm taking you there for me, not anyone else. Just be yourself, and the night will go just fine."

Salina smiled softly, but Jake could tell that she was anxious. He wanted this time with her. The event itself was secondary to him. He wanted the trip away with her, so they could have another amazing night together.

The heritage celebration would be at the Hyatt Regency, but Jake would book a suite for himself and Salina at the Four Seasons. They would make an appearance at the event but leave early, and have their own special dessert in their suite.

His mother had been getting on his case about making up his mind about a political career, pointing out that if he was going to enter the political arena, now was the time to do so. Going to this event would satisfy his mother and maybe help him decide once and for all if he would enter politics. But Jake was already leaning toward a certain decision, because it was becoming more and more clear to him that a normal family life was what he craved.

When he looked back on his own life, he had to acknowledge that something had been missing when he was growing up. And it wasn't just because he didn't have any brothers or sisters. It was because his parents had always been so involved in politics, in putting on just the right face for the public, that Jake had never quite felt that they were ever a normal family. His father wouldn't simply get up and do something—he had to first decide how it would look to the public. Every decision had been made with the public in mind.

Jake didn't want that kind of a life for Riquet; but because he hadn't yet made up his mind entirely, he would go to the event and show his face as his mother desired, make the rounds with all the right people. It would bode well for him and any future political ambition he might pursue. And of course, he would help to support a good cause.

The icing on the cake would be spending the night with Salina.

The two of them alone again, without having to worry

that Riquet might hear them, or worse, walk into his room unexpected. Jake could hardly wait.

"So we're going to fly out Friday night and return when?"

"We can make a weekend of it. Return on Sunday."

"Are you sure?" Salina asked. "I mean, do you want to be away from Riquet for two…"

Salina stopped talking, her question ending on a sigh, when Jake leaned forward and nibbled on her earlobe. "Yes, I'm sure."

Salina shuddered, and Jake remembered all too well how her body had quivered beneath his as they'd made love the previous Saturday night. He couldn't wait to have her naked and moaning in his arms once again.

"Say yes and I'll book the flight tomorrow," Jake said.

"Yes," Salina said, smiling tentatively. Then she beamed. "Yes!"

Her smile was infectious, lighting him up from the inside. For the first time since Janine's death, Jake was looking forward to going to an event.

He couldn't help thinking about what his mother might say, however. She had asked him about his involvement with Salina, and he'd told her that there was no involvement. She would soon learn otherwise.

But she would have to learn about their relationship at some point, and why not this weekend? Something was growing between he and Salina, something Jake was powerless to stop. And he didn't want to stop it. With her in his life, he had been happier than in the past two years. The trip to Baxter's farm had been a highlight for him, and also for Riquet. Jake wanted more times like that with Salina. More time with her and Riquet as a family.

And more time with her as a lover.

"Oh, my goodness," Salina suddenly said, "I have nothing to wear."

"I will take care of that."

Salina gave him an odd look. *"You?"*

"Not me personally, but I'll cover the expense for you to buy any dress you like. I'll have Ed take you to whatever stores you like. Down on Soho or on Fifth Avenue, wherever. Pick out anything you want—the dress, accessories. Then I'll arrange to pick up the tab."

"Are you serious?"

"I know better than to joke when it comes to women and shopping."

At the spark in Salina's eyes, Jake felt something tug at his chest. He remembered how much fun it had been to send Janine on a shopping trip. The first time he had let her go to a store and pick out whatever she wanted, she had stared at him with wide eyes. And the night that followed had been incredible.

But he didn't want to think about Janine right now. Now was the time for him and Salina.

"But what if I don't pick a dress that's appropriate?"

"Impossible. The most important part of the whole dress is *you.* And you are stunning. No matter what you choose, you'll look phenomenal."

Salina squealed and then threw her arms around Jake's neck. The next instant, they were kissing passionately.

Despite the heat spreading through his body, the raw desire for this beautiful woman who was in his arms, Jake broke the kiss and pulled away from her.

"Friday night," he told her. "Friday night, I'm all yours."

Chapter 18

Salina and Jake left on a four o'clock flight Friday afternoon, and by five-thirty their plane had touched down in the nation's capital. Now they were at the Four Seasons hotel in a suite that was the epitome of opulence. Their suite was a corner unit with lots of windows that would let in a lot of natural light in the day. The living room was huge, with three large and comfortable sofas. The suite also had a large dining table with an exquisite crystal chandelier above it. There was a writing desk and fax machine, as well as a flat-screen television that had to be at least forty inches.

But the oversize dressing area was a woman's dream, and that's where Salina was now, getting dressed in the designer gown she had picked up for tonight's event.

Salina's dress was a rich burgundy color with a jewel-encrusted front wrapping around the torso area. She wore drop diamond earrings to match the look of the jewels on the floor-length gown. The front came down in a V shape over her breasts, while the back was a low U-shaped scoop.

Jake walked up behind her, placed his hands on her shoulders and met her gaze in the floor-to-ceiling mirror. He whistled. "Wow. You look...you look incredible."

"You think so?" Salina asked, beaming.

"You're absolutely stunning."

"You look gorgeous yourself. Sexier than any male model." And he did. With his Armani suit that fit him immaculately, Jake looked like a million dollars.

"I'd love nothing more than to make love to you right now," Jake whispered into her ear. "But the event is going to start in about forty-five minutes."

Salina was glad they hadn't fallen into bed for a quickie before they'd started to get ready. As much as she wanted to, she knew that drawing out their desire for each other during the event would intensify their lovemaking later. Besides, she'd had her hair professionally done in soft drop curls—and she wasn't about to mess up her style before this important event.

"Later," Salina said, and turned in his arms to face him. "Later, will be worth the wait."

A little over an hour later, Salina and Jake were at the Hyatt Regency, mingling with the crowd in the ballroom. Despite the fact that Salina was wearing a designer gown and knew she looked fantastic, she felt a little out of place. All around her were important people. People of obvious wealth and stature. She recognized many political faces she'd seen on television, and couldn't help being a bit intimidated.

She stayed close to Jake, meeting and greeting people with him. As she watched him interact with those he came into contact with, she was fascinated by his natural charm and charisma. People were drawn to him. He had an easy smile and a manner that set people at ease.

In fact, this Jake was a completely different person than

the one Salina had met for the very first time at the fundraiser she had attended with her sister. That Jake had been brooding and clearly hadn't been interested in socializing. This Jake was more than outgoing, smiling and talking to everyone around him with interest. There was no doubt that he could do well in a political career.

Salina was holding her own—until the first question about what she did for a living. As it was occurring to her that perhaps she shouldn't say she was Jake's nanny, Jake spoke.

"Salina is a very talented up-and-coming chef," he explained to the woman they were speaking to, someone who worked for the White House's press office. "She will definitely have her own restaurant—or restaurants—one day."

"Ahh," the woman said, smiling brightly. "Fine dining?"

"Yes, definitely," Salina answered.

"Then I look forward to eating at your restaurant one day in the future."

Uplifted by the comment, Salina nodded graciously. Then she turned, gazing around the room. That's when she saw Jake's mother, Bernice. She was standing with a fair-skinned older gentleman, and a younger woman so beautiful she could easily have competed in pageants.

As if Bernice sensed Salina's eyes on her, she suddenly looked in her direction. Jake's mother's face definitely went from happy to stunned when she realized that Salina was in the room.

"Ah, there are my parents," Jake said, and resting his hand on Salina's elbow, began to guide her in that direction. His parents also began to walk toward them, meeting them halfway.

"Salina, you've already met my mother, Bernice, but this is my father, Albert."

"Hello, Mr. McKnight," Salina said.

"You call me Mr. McKnight, and I think my father's in the room," the man said, then chuckled at his joke.

"Albert, then," Salina said.

He took her hand in his. His eyes were bright, his smile genuine, and it was easy to see where Jake got his charisma. "That's better. I'm very pleased to meet you, Salina."

"Likewise," Salina said. Then she turned to Bernice. "Hello, Bernice."

"We meet again." Bernice turned to her son. "Jake, you never said you were bringing your nanny. Who's watching Riquet?"

"It's taken care of, Mom. You don't need to worry." Jake slipped his arm around Salina's waist. "You ready to head to our table?"

"Sure. It looks like most people are getting ready to sit down."

Jake guided Salina to the front right area of the room, where table six was marked. As he walked with her, Salina noticed the striking woman who'd been speaking with Bernice heading in their direction. A few seconds later, Salina's heart began to beat faster as she realized that the woman was actually heading for Jake.

The woman opened her arms, inviting Jake into an embrace. "Jake," she said, stretching his name into three beats. "I'm so glad you could make it. It's nice to see you again… and so soon after the last time."

The last time?

"Evening, Elizabeth," Jake said as he stepped backward from her.

Elizabeth looked in Salina's direction, her eyes widening slightly, as if she was seeing her for the first time. "Oh, hello. Jake, who's your friend?"

"Elizabeth, this is Salina. Salina, this is a friend of mine, Elizabeth."

Elizabeth and Salina shook hands. Then Elizabeth's eyes narrowed, as though in recognition, as she stared at her. "Oh, you're Jake's new nanny!"

Salina nodded.

"I heard what happened to Maria's mother." She pressed a hand to her heart. "Oh, so sad. My heart goes out to Maria. She's such a wonderful person."

Salina shot Jake a sidelong glance. Clearly, Elizabeth wasn't just a casual friend. "How do you know each other?" she couldn't help asking.

Jake looked a little uncomfortable. "Elizabeth and I dated once."

Elizabeth laughed airily and patted Jake on the chest. "He means I was once his girlfriend," she clarified. "Not that we only dated one time."

Jake had dated this woman? The reality caused Salina to feel a spurt of panic.

"We were just heading to our table," Jake told Elizabeth. "Excuse us."

Salina was happy to be rid of Elizabeth—until it turned out that she was also seated at their table. Salina was seated on Jake's left, and Elizabeth seated herself on his right.

Throughout the appetizer and the salad, Elizabeth chatted almost nonstop with Jake, smiling and laughing in a way that was clearly flirtatious. The woman's behavior was out of line—beyond disrespectful.

The only bright spot was Albert, who was seated on Salina's left. He regaled Salina with stories of his days as a pastor in Georgia, and also about his life in public office.

There were spectacular performances during dinner which included an African dance troop, as well as a youth steel band from a local high school, that elicited cheers from everyone. Salina glanced at Elizabeth, who had her body angled toward Jake and was talking to him about some events she was planning for some group she was volunteering with.

If anyone were to look at Jake and Elizabeth, they might mistakenly believe *they* had come together.

Once Salina was finished with her main course, she excused herself from the table and went to the ladies' room. She stayed in the stall longer than she needed to, taking a long moment to collect herself.

So what if Elizabeth dated Jake before? she asked herself. *He's here with me, not her. Let her flirt all she wants with him. Jake is heading back to the hotel with me tonight.*

Feeling better, Salina exited the stall. She washed her hands and was on her way to the exit when the door opened and Bernice appeared.

Salina halted, startled. But then she smiled. "Have they started the awards yet?"

"Not yet," Bernice replied. Then, "Salina, can I speak with you for a moment?"

"Sure," Salina said, wondering why on earth Bernice wanted to talk to her.

Jake's mother gestured to the restroom's comfortable seating area, which was unoccupied.

Salina headed in that direction and Bernice followed her. By the time Salina turned to face Jake's mother, she began to speak.

"I'm going to get to the point. My son is hurting right now. He's very vulnerable, and I don't want to see him taken advantage of."

Salina's mouth fell open in shock as she stared at the woman. She hadn't expected this from Jake's mother. "You think I'm taking advantage of him?"

"I'm not saying that is your intention," Bernice said. "But by getting involved with him, the result is the same. You're taking advantage of his vulnerable state of mind. And the last thing I want to see is my son hurting more than he already is."

"With all due respect, I disagree. I care about your son. I'm trying to be there for him in every way. I want to help him, not hurt him."

"You've known my son how long? Three weeks?" She raised an eyebrow, as if to say that wasn't nearly enough time. "Has he talked to you about his late wife?"

"A little, yes."

"He was *very* in love with Janine. They were the perfect couple. Inseparable. I've never seen two people more in love, and that's saying a lot. He worshiped Janine. And she worshiped him."

"I…yes, I realize that."

"Good," Bernice said, relieved. "So you understand what I'm trying to say."

"Not really," Salina told her.

"You're here at this event. That alone tells me that something is going on between the two of you. And I could see in your eyes that you were smitten with him the very first time I met you. I can't blame you. Jake is a very attractive man. Very successful, ambitious, a loving father."

"I hope you don't think that I'm only interested in your son because of his success," Salina said, hoping to put Bernice's mind at ease in case she didn't trust Salina's motives.

Bernice chuckled softly. "Oh, I'm not saying that. What I'm saying is that I understand my son is a good catch. As I already told you, I don't blame you for your interest in him, but I have to respectfully ask that you back off."

The words were like a slap. "Back off?"

"You said yourself that you understand just how much Jake was in love with Janine. The timing isn't right for him to get involved with anyone else…especially not under suspicious circumstances."

"I'm sorry?" Salina was confused.

"I don't know if he's discussed his political goals with you, but he has to be very careful about his reputation now."

"So I wouldn't be good for his reputation," Salina concluded, frowning slightly.

"I'm trying to spare your feelings," Bernice said, a hint of pity in her voice. "My son doesn't need to get involved in a relationship that will go nowhere. I can see why he would be seduced by someone like you. Simply because of the proximity. You've been living in his apartment, seeing him every day…and you're obviously a beautiful woman. But you can't be naive enough to confuse lust with love."

Salina's jaw flinched. She wanted to be respectful to Jake's mother, but never in her life had a woman spoken to her the way that Bernice had. "Lust on whose part? Mine or Jake's?"

Bernice made a sound of derision, then forced a smile at two women who entered the bathroom.

"You understand what I'm saying to you," Bernice said in a lowered voice.

"So you feel you have to have this conversation with me because you think your son's not able to figure out for himself what he feels for me?"

Now Bernice's face hardened. "I'm asking you to respect his situation. Respect that he's not ready for a relationship. You're only setting yourself up for heartbreak. I saw him with Janine. The way his face lit up every time he was with her. I could *feel* the love between them. I don't want to burst your bubble, but I see nothing that compares to that when Jake looks at you. Do yourself a favor…exit Jake's life before you're in too deep. If not for Jake, then have the decency to think about Riquet."

Bernice turned and walked away then, leaving Salina standing in the vanity area of the bathroom dumbfounded.

Her parting shot had hurt her more than she would have believed possible.

Riquet… Would Riquet end up crushed if Salina and Jake parted ways? Lord knew, Salina didn't want to hurt that precious little girl. She had come to love her, just as she loved her dad.

As much as Salina told herself that that she shouldn't be affected by Bernice's words, she couldn't help it. The words stung.

Yes, Salina knew that Jake had adored his wife. Yes, she had been worried about the possibility that he might not have his whole heart to give. And yet Jake had made love to her like no other man ever had. That had to mean something. Salina was sure of that. She wasn't delusional. She wasn't simply hoping that sexual attraction meant love.

Jake cared for her deeply. He had proved that in the bedroom…*and* outside of it.

I'm not deluding myself. I'm not setting myself up for heartbreak. Jake is attracted to me. I know he is.

But what if Bernice was right? What if Salina was simply a distraction for Jake? A pleasant distraction for the time being, but ultimately not someone he would love forever?

As a group of beautifully dressed women entered the bathroom chatting happily, Salina went to the sink and splashed some cold water on her face. She stood there for a moment, her heart racing, and then she dried off and exited the bathroom.

She was heading back into the ballroom when she spotted Jake from behind. He was heading up the stairs.

And he wasn't alone.

Elizabeth, that annoying woman who had been flirting with him all night, was walking up the staircase ahead of him.

Salina couldn't miss the woman's bright red formfitting dress.

Her stomach twisting, Salina watched as they reached the top step. She continued to watch in horror as the man she loved and his ex-girlfriend turned to the right and disappeared out of view.

Chapter 19

"All right," Jake said as he and Elizabeth reached a far corner of the hotel's lobby level where he was certain they would have some privacy. "You said you wanted a quiet place to talk. This is as good as any."

"I want to be sure we're away from prying eyes."

Jake clenched his jaw and watched as Elizabeth opened the door to a disabled restroom. "Elizabeth," he began in protest.

"You want people to see us standing off in the corner and jump to assumptions?" she challenged. Her eyes were darting left and right beyond him, to see if the way was clear.

Jake hated to admit that she was right. "Fine," he said, and after a quick look behind, to see that no curious onlookers were in the vicinity, he followed her into the large, open bathroom.

She had requested that they talk privately, and Jake had agreed because he wanted to tell her to knock it off with all of her excessive flirting. Explain to her once and for all that there was no hope of a future relationship between them. But he didn't want to embarrass her, so doing so in private was optimal.

"Okay," he began when the door was closed. "What was so important that you needed to speak with me alone?" He would let her talk first, then get to the issue he wanted to address.

"This," Elizabeth said. And then without warning, she advanced, wrapping her arms around his neck and kissing him.

Anger burned hotly in Jake's veins. He gripped Elizabeth by her shoulders and wrenched her off him. "For God's sake, what are you doing?"

"Helping you remember. Helping you remember what we had."

She moved toward him again, but Jake put out a hand to hold her at bay. "Stop right there," he said. "I'm here with someone, for crying out loud."

Elizabeth rolled her eyes. "Salina?"

"And even if I weren't, I'm not interested in you." He paused, held her gaze, hoping she would see that he was deadly serious.

"You and I were great together. We can be great together again. You just have to give us a chance."

"Not gonna happen. And at this rate, I am remembering why I'm not even in touch with you. It's all too clear that we can't even be friends."

Elizabeth said nothing, but Jake saw her swallow. "You're right, Jake. We can't be friends. We've tried and it doesn't work—because I want everything with you." She paused briefly. "I always thought that after a while you'd come to me. See the light and realize I was always the one for you.

When you were still grieving, I gave you your space. Now you start seeing some nobody nanny instead of *me?*"

"We dated a very long time ago."

"I'm still in love with you," Elizabeth said, her tone softer now, her voice sounding as though she was going to cry. "Why do you hate me so much?"

Jake drew in a deep breath and expelled it slowly. Perhaps he needed to try a different tactic. "Elizabeth," he began gently, "I don't hate you. And I'd like for us to be friends. But that means you can't hit on me, you can't disrespect me, you—"

"I'm just supposed to stand by and watch you and Salina get involved," she quipped, her tone saying the idea was ludicrous.

"Yes," Jake said softly.

Something stirred in Elizabeth's eyes. Something dark. "Are you really that blind? Are you so blind that you can't see you're making the wrong choice—again?"

"Whomever I get involved with is none of your business, Elizabeth. We're over. Get that through your head."

"Even your mother can see that you're heading down a disastrous road."

"I've tried to be nice," Jake said, exasperated, "but clearly we're done here."

"You thought that Janine was your perfect soul mate," Elizabeth went on, undeterred. "Was that why she was so quick to believe secrets others told her about you?"

Jake's chest tightened. "What?"

"The day she got into the crash. Your precious Janine was on her way to hear all the sordid details about you."

Anger consumed Jake. He wanted to wring Elizabeth's neck for the lie. "You're lying."

She gave him a smug smile. And then she said, "Of course. You'd never believe your precious Janine had any faults. On the other hand, how much did your wife trust you? Not very much, it turns out."

Jake should have left the bathroom already. He knew Elizabeth was talking nonsense. She was trying to fill his head with poison—whatever garbage would stick.

And yet there was something…something about her mentioning Janine that made him suddenly want to hear her out. See exactly what she had to say.

"Janine knew she could trust me," Jake said.

"Did she?"

"Of course she did."

"Then why was it that when I called her, told her that I needed to talk to her about *you*—she came running?"

Jake stared at Elizabeth, trying to gauge if this was yet another lie. Elizabeth was so bitter over the fact that he had chosen Janine and not her, that he couldn't trust her completely. She would say anything to get to him now, because he was once again rejecting her.

"Janine trusted me," Jake reiterated.

"I told her that you'd been unfaithful to her. That I was sorry about our relationship and wanted to talk to her about it. She got in her car immediately and came to me. What does that tell you?"

Jake balled his hands into fists. He almost wanted to grab Elizabeth and shake her until that arrogant smile was erased from her face. "Are you telling me you called Janine?"

"I'm telling you that your fantasy of the perfect marriage is a lie. If your wife trusted you so much, she never would've come to see me."

Jake pounded the wall beside Elizabeth's head and she yelped. As much as he knew that there would be some satisfaction in throttling her, he would never touch a woman.

But he stared down at Elizabeth with what he knew was

a lethal expression. "You called my wife? You told her I was having an affair with you?" He had to be sure. "You met with her and spun a web of lies?"

"She never made it to me," Elizabeth said, seeming to look a bit more contrite now. "She…she crashed en route. My only goal was to prove something to you. I wanted to show you that she didn't trust you the way you thought she did. That's why she wasn't perfect for you. I, on the other hand, would have trusted—"

"Shut up!" Jake yelled. He began to pace the floor in the small bathroom, dragging a hand over his head. As the seconds passed, he digested this news—and knew it was true.

Stopping at one of the bathroom walls, he splayed his hands on the wallpapered surface and tightly closed his eyes. His heart nearly imploded with the reality of what he had just heard. He had always known that something was off that day. Janine had out of the blue told him that she wanted to head out to her parents, and he hadn't objected, but he had sensed that there was something wrong. That there was something else going on. That perhaps she had been upset with him for some reason that she hadn't wanted to say.

To think that Elizabeth had actually lured her out of the home as a way to try to destroy his marriage—and as a result, Janine had ended up in a fatal accident—Elizabeth was the lowliest of the low.

And she actually had the audacity to be more interested in proving that Janine hadn't been the perfect wife, rather than expressing any regret over the fact that her lie had cost Janine her life.

Jake spun around and faced her. "I despise you." He spoke clearly so there would be no misunderstanding. "It was a mistake to ever get involved with you. You sucked me in with your lies and charm, but when I met Janine I realized what a true woman was. Why do you think I dumped you so unexpectedly? Because I'd met Janine and knew instantly that she was the woman for me." He was using words to hurt her. Words that he knew would devastate her. This was how he would get to her, and it would be more hurtful than any physical blow.

Elizabeth looked crestfallen, but Jake didn't stop. "You never even came close to being the kind of woman she was. I had to leave you once I met her—because she was everything I wanted, not you."

Jake paused, saw that Elizabeth's eyes were filling with tears. "You were merely something to pass the time with while I was bored," Jake finished, knowing that his final words would strike the most powerful blow.

Then he headed to the door, finished with Elizabeth once and for all.

"She's wrong for you!" Elizabeth cried out. "You'll see!"

Jake had nothing more to say to her. He placed his hand on the doorknob.

"Jake!" Elizabeth screamed, her voice ripe with tears.

Finally Jake turned. He saw a little light come on in Elizabeth's eyes. Her chest rose and fell as she breathed in unsteadily, clearly fighting to prevent more tears from falling down her face.

Jake knew that he could at this moment take back what he'd said—at least ease the pain somewhat, given her emotional state. But that was the last thing Elizabeth deserved. So Jake said, "It doesn't matter who's right or wrong for me. It only matters that you are the last woman on earth I would ever touch. If I had to choose death or you—I would choose death. No contest."

Then Jake pulled open the door and stalked off, leaving Elizabeth sobbing uncontrollably.

* * *

Satisfaction over what he'd said to Elizabeth didn't last long. Because his own heart was breaking, knowing that Janine's death was all the more senseless.

Elizabeth had called his wife out of the home for a bogus reason, and that had cost her her life.

Jake would never forgive Elizabeth.

But would he ever forgive himself?

He went back downstairs and to the ballroom, where he headed for his table. He was done with this event. He was going to get Salina and leave. The last thing he was going to do was sit next to Elizabeth for another second, much less the next hour and a half.

Only, when he got to the table he saw that Salina was not there. He glanced around quickly but saw her nowhere within the vicinity.

"Son," Bernice began, "Salina asked me to tell you that she's leaving."

Jake's heart spasmed. "What?"

"She said she wasn't feeling well and that she was heading back to the hotel."

Jake immediately turned and started striding back toward the ballroom's exit. Unfortunately, Elizabeth was on her way in and he had to pass her. He noted that, though she had cried off most of her makeup, you would never know she had been in a state of emotional distress only a short time before. She had plastered on a fake smile to appear to the world that she was just fine.

And her world would no doubt be just fine, but Jake's world had forever been altered.

Jake went back to the hotel immediately, but found the suite empty. He hoped that perhaps Salina was out somewhere, like at a store, or taking a walk. But the truth became obvious when he saw the note on the bed in the bedroom, beside the gown she'd been wearing.

> Dear Jake,
> I apologize for leaving so suddenly, but I had to.
> I have rearranged my flight and am heading back to New York tonight.
> I'm sure this will be a surprise to you. Then again, maybe not. We can talk when you get home. But I want you to know that I am tendering my resignation. I will stay for the rest of the week. That should be enough time for you to find a replacement nanny.
> Salina

Jake reread the note in a state of disbelief. He went for his BlackBerry to call Salina. He went as far as to dial her number.

But he didn't complete the call.

He didn't know what had caused Salina's abrupt decision, but there was one thing he suddenly couldn't deny—it was best that they end whatever relationship they had started.

It was all too clear to Jake that he had to accept the blame for Janine's death, and that was hard to deal with. Because if he accepted the blame, then that meant he had to accept the guilt.

If only he had told Janine about Elizabeth, Janine would have known that Elizabeth was a cold and calculating liar when she'd called her. Instead, Janine had doubted him. She had doubted him because he had not been around enough to give her the attention she needed.

Jake was responsible for her death. He hadn't killed her, no. But if he had been a better husband she would likely still be alive today.

Jake sank onto the bed and glanced at the evening gown

Salina had been wearing. He had hoped to end the night making incredible love to her all night long. Instead she had left him.

It hurt. Lord knew that it did. But it was for the best.

Because for failing Janine, Jake deserved to be alone.

Chapter 20

Salina felt bad about the way she had changed her first class ticket and left Washington—and Jake—without an explanation, and back at his apartment she was in an emotional slump. Riquet was at the babysitter's, and Salina certainly could have gone to her sister's place, but she wasn't in the mood to see Emma and answer the questions that her sister no doubt would have about what had happened between her and Jake.

She wanted—needed—some time alone to collect her thoughts.

Besides, she also expected Jake to return the next day—possibly on an earlier flight, given that she had left him—and she knew they needed to have a talk. Also, she meant what she had written in her note. She intended to finish her week as Riquet's nanny as she had told him she would.

Sitting up on the bed, hugging a pillow, Salina felt a mix of emotions. She was looking forward to seeing Riquet the next day, but she also felt sad about the fact that her time with the young girl was coming to an end.

She had come to love Riquet, she truly had, and she was going to miss being a part of the girl's life.

But being a part of Riquet's life meant she also had to be a part of Jake's life. There could be no middle ground. For Salina, it was all or nothing.

And that's why it was best that she cut her ties with Jake once and for all. Speaking with his mother had driven that point home. Bernice had told her in no uncertain terms that she wasn't good enough for Jake. And not only that, she had assured her that Jake would never love her the way he had loved Janine.

It confirmed Salina's biggest fears. That she was deluding herself where Jake was concerned. She was in love with him, but he would never return her feelings—at least not wholly and completely, which was what Salina required. She couldn't settle for second best, take the half of Jake's heart that he was possibly able to give.

Yes, they had been having a wonderful time lately, but just as before, he would no doubt put up his walls again. The longer Salina stayed involved with him, the more devastated she would be in the long run.

So it was best this way. End things now and move on with her heart still intact.

Not to mention the disturbing fact that she had seen him disappear with his ex-girlfriend. At the sight of the two of them together, disappearing up the stairs, her heart had felt as though someone had put it in a vise and squeezed.

She didn't even want to imagine what that was about. But just looking at Elizabeth, it was plain to see that she fit into the political scene with ease.

Gorgeous, polished and sophisticated, she would be the perfect political wife.

Salina had made her decision, and yet the very idea of moving on filled her with the most intense sorrow. She couldn't remember ever feeling this crushed when breaking up with someone before.

Still holding the pillow, she lay back on her bed in Jake's apartment. The place was quiet, emphasizing the fact that she was alone. And alone she could no longer hold back the tears. She cried and cried—hoping to rid her system of Jake McKnight by the time he returned and they had the talk she knew they needed to have.

That conversation came the next day around three o'clock when Jake returned.

Salina was in her bedroom lying down, in hope of getting some sleep, since she had barely slept the night before, when there was a knock on her door. She sat up, her heart beginning to beat rapidly at the realization that Jake was home.

"Salina? Are you in there?"

"Yes," Salina answered. "You can come in."

Jake opened the door and Salina drew in a sharp breath at the sight of him. She had spent the entire night telling herself that she could get over him easily, but seeing him now made it clear that the task would be harder than she had imagined.

There was just something about him that spoke to her heart. He looked incredibly sexy, even though the expression on his face was conflicted. She wanted with all her might to reach out to him and make all of his pain go away.

If only her love could make him heal….

But Salina knew better.

"You left," Jake said without preamble. He stepped into the room, stopping about halfway between the door and the bed.

"I didn't think you would miss me."

Jake gave her a quizzical stare. "Pardon me?"

"You had Elizabeth to keep you company," Salina said, the words burning in her throat as she spoke them.

Jake's mouth fell open. Clearly he didn't consider that Salina had seen the two of them together.

"I saw you two disappear up the stairs," Salina supplied. "When you were gone a ridiculously long time I thought, *Why am I here?* But I figured that at least, if you returned when I was getting my coat, I wouldn't look like a total fool. You didn't."

"It's not what you think."

"Where did you go? To her hotel room?"

"No." Jake took a step closer to the bed, then stopped. "Definitely not."

"I can't believe you would bring me all the way to DC and embarrass me by taking off with someone else."

"I needed to talk to Elizabeth about something impor—"

"Oh, I'm sure you did."

Jake walked closer to the bed but didn't sit down. "Elizabeth is a parasite. Trust me on that. If you'll let me tell you—"

"I think I've had my fill of talks." And though Salina had planned on having this chat with Jake, her chest was constricting so badly that all she wanted to do was avoid this unpleasant moment. She didn't want to talk about how they didn't have a future. She simply wanted to be gone.

"But we're not talking," Jake said, clearly confused.

"I may as well tell you that your mother spoke to me. She gave me an earful last night."

"Damn it," Jake muttered. Finally he eased himself down on the bed.

Salina's pulse quickened. She wanted to feel nothing being this close to Jake, but her body was betraying her. And so was her heart.

"I learned something last night," Jake began, "about Elizabeth. About my late wife." He expelled a ragged breath. "Suffice it to say I never want to see Elizabeth again as long as I live. The last thing you have to worry about is me being involved with her. I despise the woman."

The words gave Salina pause. Jake's words, plus his demeanor, made it clear that something serious had happened between him and Elizabeth. Something that must have involved his late wife.

Did Salina dare ask him? Did she get herself further involved with this man, when she had already decided that they couldn't be together?

"What did my mother say to you? Although I can imagine."

"She made some things perfectly clear. That I'm not the woman for you. That people would see a relationship with me as a flaw in your character because I'm your nanny— and that would come back to bite you if you ever were in political office." Salina stopped, paused. "That you'll never love me the way you loved your wife." She met Jake's eyes as she said these last words, hoping that he would tell her his mother had been wrong.

Instead he sighed. "My mother had no right. No right to talk to you about our relationship. She was excessively rude, and for that I apologize."

And…? Was that all he had to say? A lump lodged in Salina's throat, large and painful.

"Salina," Jake began softly, "I first want to say that I have enjoyed getting to know you, spending intimate time with you—"

"Please, spare me." Salina looked away, trying to hold in her tears.

"I realize you're unhappy with me, but I've tried to explain to you about last night. At the end of the day, you were the one who left me in DC."

"Because a lot of things became obvious to me," Salina said, her eyes filling with tears. "Between your mother, and Elizabeth…"

"I'm sorry," Jake said. "I'm sorry you had an awful night. I don't blame you for leaving."

But. Salina knew there was one.

"But I think you came to the same conclusion that I did. That we should end things now. We got caught up in something… But even if it's over I'm hoping we can be friends."

"So you felt nothing for me? We just got *caught up* in something?"

Salina saw Jake's Adam's apple rise and fall. "I…I didn't say I felt nothing."

"I know I left you in Washington, and I can admit that was the wrong thing to do. Between your mother and Elizabeth, I was overwhelmed. And I don't deny that your mother's words got to me, made me fear that you would never love me the way you loved Janine. And yes, I started to think that maybe we were better off going our separate ways. But not because I think that we just *fell into something.* So please have more respect for me than that, and let's have a real conversation here."

"All right. I think…" Jake's voice trailed off. "I think you deserve better…than me. Than what I have to offer."

That wasn't the answer Salina expected to hear. She could see the pain in Jake's eyes as he spoke the words, hear it in his voice. "Jake?" She reached out and touched his arm. "Why would you say that?"

"I had my chance. It failed. You deserve a man who doesn't have the baggage that I do."

"So, because you were married before you don't deserve to be happy again?"

Jake stood. "It's complicated."

"That's all you have to say?"

Salina stared up at Jake, waiting for him to answer. He said nothing.

"Answer me!" she shouted. She hadn't meant to raise her voice, but Jake was breaking her heart. It was all too clear to her that she wasn't saving herself from heartbreak by walking away now. She was already in too deep.

"I don't know what to say," Jake said softly.

"I said I wanted you to be real with me. Did you not feel what I did when we made love? Was it not special to you at all?"

"Of course it was. God, Salina…you have no idea."

"So what happened?"

Jake paused. Then he said, "Life. Life happened."

Salina jumped up from the bed and stood before him. "This is why I left you in Washington. Because I feared you were going to put the walls up again. And that's exactly what you're doing."

"I thought I could do this," Jake said. "But I can't. I…I can't. I loved someone. I lost her. That was my one chance and I blew it."

Salina stared at him in confusion. And instead of her pain, she tried to dissect his words.

Something had happened last night. He'd learned something that had hurt him. She was certain of that. Something that was adding to his sense of guilt.

"What do you mean you blew it?" she asked.

"Please stop asking me questions. Just…just respect what I'm saying."

Something more was going on. Salina was sure of it. And now she wished that she had let Jake finish what he'd been starting to say about Elizabeth. "What did Elizabeth say to you?"

"I care for you," Jake said, not answering her question. "I care for you enough to let you know that I'm not sure I have my whole heart to give right now. And if I can't give you my whole heart, is it fair to expect you to stick around? I have to let you go so you can find someone else."

The words were like a stab in the heart. How could he say that to her? How, after the incredible nights they'd spent making love, could he actually believe that?

"I don't believe a word you just said. I know what we shared. And so do you. I know you're scared. Maybe you're afraid of loving and losing someone else. Are you going to live your life alone, simply because you're afraid of caring for another person?"

"You tendered your resignation and I accept it," Jake said, and started for the door.

Salina stared at Jake in dismay. Oh, God. Her heart. How was it that she had come to care so deeply for him in such a short time?

"So that's it?" Salina asked, speaking to his back. "You're just going to walk away?"

"Yes."

Jake didn't turn as he reached the door. He simply walked out of her room, leaving Salina devastated and alone.

Jake felt like crap as he headed to his bedroom. But he'd had to get away from Salina. Get away from her before he caved to the selfish desire to take her in his arms, hold her and never let her go.

He hadn't been entirely honest with her, and he knew she was confused. He had let her believe that he was ending things because he was afraid to love, and he couldn't deny that that was a part of his reality. Yes, he knew firsthand how devastating life could be. One day you could have the person you loved with you, and the next they were gone.

But he also couldn't deny that he had found something

special with Salina. Something real. It didn't matter that he'd known her only weeks. Their connection was the real thing.

The one time in his life that he had fallen for someone quickly had been when he'd met Janine, and he had known then that it was the real thing, as well. In fact, there was a part of Jake that believed the connection he felt with Salina was perhaps even greater than the one he'd had with Janine.

But none of that mattered. Because knowing the truth about how Janine had died was killing him.

He had to accept that if he'd been a better husband she would still be alive. And that was a bitter pill to swallow.

Sadly, Elizabeth's actions weren't illegal. Which meant she couldn't go to jail for Janine's death. At the end of the day, it had been a tragic accident.

But with Elizabeth still at large and still obsessing over him, she was clearly unpredictable. Her call to Janine had indirectly led to her death. How would she try to infect Salina's life as a way to lash out at her?

Because, if Elizabeth hurt Salina…Jake would never forgive himself if something happened to Salina, too.

Jake could handle being alone forever…as long as it meant that Salina would be safe from Elizabeth's volatile wrath.

Because if he lost Salina to tragedy, too, how could he possibly go on? How could a man suffer two heartbreaking losses in his lifetime? Wouldn't it be better for him to simply continue with his life as it was? To have Maria return as his nanny, and to have his work as his focus and his life back to the way it had been before?

Jake heard the apartment door open and knew that Salina had left. He assumed she was coming back… Riquet was due to return with Lisa at six o'clock, and Salina had promised to finish out the week.

It's best this way, Jake told himself. *She'll get over the hurt soon enough. She'll move on.*

But the thought didn't truly give Jake any comfort. As he lay on his bed, all he could do was think about her and the amazing connection they had. Both emotional and physical.

She was vibrant, spontaneous and she challenged him in a way that Janine never had. And her laugh…God, that laugh was simply wonderful. The kind that filled a room with warmth.

Filled his heart with warmth…

There was a radiance about Salina, the kind that lit up a room, something he'd noticed about her the very first time he'd met her.

He'd fallen in love with her. He knew that.

He would always have a special place in his heart for Janine. She was the mother of his child, and if she were alive today, there was no way that he would ever be with anyone else. But that said, he had found something with Salina he hadn't expected to find.

But when you loved someone you had to be selfless. You had to set them free if that was the best thing for them.

As much as Jake knew that he loved her, he also knew that he would never forgive himself for failing Janine. And that meant he wouldn't have his whole heart to give to Salina.

So how could he lead her on, only to hurt her in the long run?

No, he had to do the right thing. Let Salina go now.

No matter how much it hurt.

Chapter 21

Salina returned to the apartment just after six, once Riquet was already home. Though Jake knew she was hurting and that she was upset with him, she put on a brave face, smiling happily when she saw Riquet, and giving his daughter the biggest of hugs. Then she and Riquet played in the living room and Jake went into his bedroom.

Riquet would think that he was working as usual, but the truth was that Jake simply couldn't bear to be with both of them, sharing more family time. That would only serve to reinforce exactly what Jake was giving up by letting Salina go.

The next day he was relieved to be back in the office and able to put some physical distance between him and Salina. He threw himself into the boxes of files from the drug company, files they were late in disclosing.

Jake had instructed his secretary not to let any calls through unless they were absolutely vital. He had a lot of work to do.

Shortly after one, Jake was eating a sandwich at his desk and still poring over files when his phone rang. He could see that the call was generating from his secretary's extension and he didn't answer it. But no sooner than the call went to voice mail, it immediately began to ring again.

Picking up the receiver, Jake said impatiently, "Sharon, I told you that I didn't want any interruptions."

"Sir, you'll want to take this call. It's serious."

Jake instantly sat up straight. "Is my daughter okay?" Although if something had happened to Riquet, wouldn't Salina have called his BlackBerry?

"There's a nurse on the line saying she needs to speak to you urgently," Sharon explained.

Jake's heart jumped into his throat. "Put her through."

And then came the words that threatened to destroy his world—again.

"Mr. McKnight, I'm calling from New York Presbyterian Hospital," a woman with a nasally voice said. "Your nanny, Salina Brown, was injured, and she's been admitted."

"She—she's in the hospital?" Jake asked. His heart was beating furiously, memories of another phone call on a winter night two years ago gripping him instantly.

"She's okay, but she's had an accident."

An accident, just like before. Oh, God… Had Ed crashed the car? Had Salina gotten hit while crossing the street?

"What kind of an accident?" Jake exclaimed.

"We'll explain everything when you get here. Are you able to come right away? Your daughter is here with no one to take care of her, and she's asking for you."

"I'm on my way."

Jake slammed the receiver back into its cradle and rolled his chair back quickly. As he grabbed his blazer from the back of his chair, the updraft caused one of the legal folders to fall to the floor, spilling all of the documents inside.

He didn't care.

He rushed out of the office, leaving his files where they were, the lawsuit the last thing on his mind. He went downstairs, hailed a cab and urgently told the driver to take him to the hospital.

Every step of the way there, his heart pounded in his chest so hard that it hurt. He was scared.

No, scared was an understatement. He was downright terrified.

What kind of accident had Salina been involved in?

Obviously, she hadn't been killed. But Janine also hadn't been killed instantly. Jake had gotten that evening call and rushed to the hospital to be at his wife's side, only to be too late. She had died while he was en route.

Jake found it hard to breathe and loosened his tie. Surely, if Salina was in very bad shape he would've detected that in the nurse's voice. And yet the nurse didn't sound particularly distressed. Still, medical professionals could be dispassionately cool, even in the face of devastating circumstances.

"Hurry, please," Jake said to the taxi driver. "I need to get to the hospital as soon as possible."

The driver pressed his foot to the gas pedal and the car surged forward. Clearly, he had detected the note of desperation in Jake's voice.

It suddenly occurred to Jake that he had rushed out of the office without speaking to Emma. If something bad had happened to Salina, Emma would certainly want to know. He dug his BlackBerry out of his pocket and punched in the digits to Emma's office extension. When her assistant answered, he barked, "This is Jake McKnight. I need to speak with Emma immediately."

A moment later Emma's line was ringing. She picked up, saying, "Jake, what's the matter?"

"I'm on my way to the hospital. I don't know what's happened, but apparently there's been an accident involving your sister. I was so worried when I got the news that I just left and didn't even think about calling you. I'm on my way to New York Presbyterian as we speak. I figured I would let you know, that you would want to come, as well."

Jake was aware that he sounded completely flustered. He was. He didn't know what to expect when he got to the hospital, and he was terrified.

Far more scared than he ever thought he would be.

And he was kicking himself for the conversation he'd had with Salina last night. Suddenly he wanted to take back everything he'd said to her. Now the idea of leaving her in order to protect her seemed utterly foolish. He wanted nothing more than to hug her and tell her that he loved her and wanted her in his life for all time.

He wanted to be the one to protect her, keep her safe to the best of his ability.

But he didn't know if it was too late.

Salina was being tended to in an emergency ward bed, a young male resident bandaging her sprained foot, when she heard a commotion outside.

"I need to see her immediately…"

Jake's voice. Nerves tickled her stomach.

The curtain blocking her bed was jerked aside and there stood Jake. The look on his face was one of absolute terror.

His eyes quickly assessed her, settling on her injured foot. He couldn't have sounded more relieved when he said, "Salina…"

"Daddy!" Riquet, who had been sitting on the chair in the small makeshift room, jumped up and ran into Jake's arms.

"Hey, honey," he said, his eyes still on Salina.

"Who are you?" the doctor asked.

"He's my employer," Salina quickly explained. "I'm his nanny."

"Salina fell down the stairs at the subway," Riquet explained.

"The subway?" Jake asked.

"Riquet wanted to ride the subway for a change," Salina explained. "Instead of going with Ed in the car. I figured, why not? Somehow I lost my footing…"

"You're okay?" Jake asked. He sounded a little breathless.

"I have a second-degree ankle sprain," Salina said, looking at the doctor for confirmation.

"Yes," the doctor agreed. "She's very lucky. She tore a ligament, but the X-rays showed no bone fracture. And if the sprain was any worse she'd need to have a cast. All she needs now is to keep her ankle wrapped, and it will heal in no time."

"She couldn't walk!" Riquet exclaimed.

Jake looked at Salina. "I…I couldn't. I couldn't put any pressure on it."

"She was brave," Riquet went on. "She only cried a little bit."

"I'll bet she was brave," Jake said softly.

"That should do it," the resident said, finishing up the bandaging. "Now, you're going to take it easy, right? And remember, *Rice*."

"Rice?" Jake asked, confused.

"Rest, ice, compression and elevation," the doctor explained.

"But I can still work, right?" Salina asked. "You said I'll have to use crutches for at least the first couple of days, but—"

"You won't be working," Jake said. "I'll call the agency and request another nanny."

Salina's heart sank. Her last week with Riquet was suddenly over.

"And I'll take care of the medical expenses," Jake went on. "To whom shall I speak about that?"

"If you go back out to the desk you passed on the way in, you can deal with that there," the resident explained.

"Good." To Salina, he said, "I'll be back shortly."

Shortly turned out to be twenty minutes later, when a nurse was in the room with her, giving her a bottle of pain medication and final instructions as to how to care for her injured foot.

The woman turned to Jake, "Are you the one taking Salina home?"

"Yes."

"Great." The woman faced Salina once more. "You're good to go."

"Where's Riquet?" Salina asked Jake.

"I had Ed pick her up," he explained. "I called my mother, and he'll be taking her there."

So she wasn't even going to get to say goodbye to Riquet. Salina swallowed, trying to keep her emotions in check.

Minutes later Salina was discharged and being transported in a wheelchair to the hospital's exit. Jake stepped outside to hail a cab, and soon he was helping her into the back of it.

They sat in the backseat, neither saying anything as the taxi pulled into traffic. Then Jake broke the silence. "I thought your sister might have shown up. I told her you were in the hospital."

"She called my cell. I told her I was okay, that she didn't need to leave the office on account of me."

Jake nodded, his expression solemn.

"Do you want the driver to take me to Brooklyn?" Salina asked tentatively. There was no reason for her to head back to Jake's apartment.

"No. Absolutely not. You'll head to my place."

Now Salina was the one to say nothing. Knowing Jake, he felt bad that she'd been injured, but if things were over between them, Salina would prefer to head home. That said, it was best this way. She could get her belongings from Jake's place, then call a taxi to take her to Brooklyn.

"How do you feel?" Jake asked her.

"A little woozy," Salina told him. "That pain medication is kicking in."

She leaned her head back in the taxi and closed her eyes... and that was the last thing she remembered.

Chapter 22

When Salina's eyelids fluttered opened she was immediately disoriented. She had no clue where she was, only the sense that she didn't know what was going on.

She blinked, looked around. And realized that she was lying on her bed in Jake's apartment.

When...how...?

She tried to move her legs, found it hard to move her right foot, and suddenly it all came back to her. Falling down the subway stairs, being in the hospital. Jake in the taxi with her.

But how had she gotten into Jake's apartment and the bed?

"Jake?" she called. Had he brought her to the apartment and then returned to work?

Moments later she heard the sound of footfalls approaching. Her bedroom door opened. "You're awake."

"Um, yeah." She glanced toward the window, saw that it was dark outside. "What time is it?"

"A little after six."

"What?" She'd slept that long?

"I think whatever medication they gave you knocked you out," Jake said softly. "Do you need anything? Some soup, tea?"

"I—I'm fine," Salina finished with difficulty, surprised to find that her voice was a little hoarse. She cleared her throat. "Well, maybe just some water."

Jake disappeared and returned a short time later with a tall glass of water. As he took a step toward her, Salina couldn't help taking in his sexy form. He was dressed in jeans and a formfitting black T-shirt, and Lord, but the man was fine.

Even at a time like this, she was feeling the pull of attraction toward him. It didn't make sense.

He passed her the glass and Salina took a long sip.

Jake eased down onto the bed beside her. His presence was overpowering. Intoxicating.

And strangely, Salina was sensing something from Jake... something in the way he was looking at her that had her wanting to forget the conversation they'd had last night.

"Anything you want, you have me get it," he said. "I'm taking the day off tomorrow to work from home, so I can be here and take care of you."

Salina raised an eyebrow, shocked. "I'm fine, Jake. You said Riquet is at your mother's. I'll be able to get around on my own. Please don't miss work because of me. In fact, if you want me to leave, head back to Brook—"

"Leave?" Jake looked at her as if she had sprouted a second nose. "You're not going anywhere. I want you totally focused on getting well. My mother will bring Riquet home tomorrow—she's very worried about you, by the way, and insisted that she be here so she can help care for you, too—and I want you to know that I'll be staying home to take care of Riquet tomorrow and the next day, so that you can get the rest you need."

"Really, Jake—I'm okay."

"Your foot is injured. It was injured because you were out with my daughter. I feel responsible."

Salina smiled softly to herself. She couldn't help thinking that Jake was acting as though he felt a lot more than "responsible." She had seen the look of panic in his eyes when he entered the hospital room, as though he expected to find her on life support. The relief on his face had been palpable, once he had learned that she merely had suffered a sprained ankle but was otherwise okay.

Jake eased over, moving closer to her, and Salina was surprised when he slipped his arm around her waist. "I suppose I'm not making myself clear," he began. "I want you here because I want you near me. Maybe you'll think I'm crazy—I'm doing a complete about-face from my position yesterday—but sometimes it's the simple things that put everything into perspective. Because your mishap—while not serious in the grand scheme of things—has made me realize that I can't let you walk out of my life…not unless you want to. I was terrified when I got the call that you were in the hospital. Absolutely terrified."

Salina had heard how upset he'd been. Emma had called her, frantic because of Jake's call to her. Salina had gone on to tell her sister that she was fine, that she'd merely suffered a sprained ankle. Salina had had the nurse call Jake, because at the time that her foot was being x-rayed, Riquet had to be taken care of by hospital staff. Clearly—at that moment anyway—she hadn't been able to fulfill her duties as nanny. Salina had simply hoped that Jake would either be able to come and get Riquet, or perhaps send Ed to pick her up.

But Jake had interpreted the call from the nurse as something far worse. Proof that Salina had been unable to call him because she had been too injured to do so.

And it was when Salina had heard from Emma just how

distraught Jake was, that hope began to burn in her heart. A small flame, but it was hope nonetheless.

It was almost worth it to have fallen and sprained her ankle, just to see this reaction from Jake.

His hands moving down her thighs, Jake said, "Give me your foot."

"Jake—"

"Give it to me," he interrupted her. "The doctor said you should keep it raised."

"It's on the bed."

"But it isn't elevated."

Salina didn't argue, just straightened her leg and extended her foot. Jake repositioned himself so that he could put her foot on his lap. "Does it still hurt a lot?"

"The pain medication is doing its job. It feels a lot better."

"Good."

Silence passed between them, and Jake began to gently massage her calf. Though that part of her leg was perfectly fine, Salina didn't complain. It felt good—good to have him touching her in any capacity.

"I'm sorry," Jake said softly.

"Jake, please don't apologize. This could have happened at any time. I simply fell."

"That's not what I mean. You didn't respond to what I said a few minutes ago, and I can understand why not. You're scared to trust me. And that's why I'm sorry—I'm sorry for being so wishy-washy concerning us. I know I've been confusing. One minute wanting you, the next pushing you away.

"The truth is…I'm in love with you. And I don't want to lose you. Today was a wake-up call. It taught me that I have to capitalize on what I have with you right now, not worry about what might happen tomorrow."

"Jake." Salina sucked in a sharp breath.

"I mean it. I'm in love with you. Trust me, that's not something I say lightly."

Salina believed it, and her eyes filled with tears. Jake was right—when he'd talked about doing an about-face minutes earlier, she hadn't responded because she'd been afraid to. Afraid that with his next breath he would reject her again.

"And not only was my mother rude, she was wrong. Falling for you has made me realize that a person can love more than one person deeply in a lifetime. My love didn't run out when I lost Janine. I still have more love to give."

Salina gently stroked his face. Those words were exactly what she'd needed to hear.

"I was running from what I felt for you. Guilt, I guess. Guilt that I was having feelings as strong for you as I'd had for Janine."

At the mention of Janine, Salina swallowed. "Jake, tell me what happened with Elizabeth last night. What did she do?"

Emotion streaked across his face, a look full of agony.

"Jake?" *Please don't shut me out...*

"Last night I learned that she told Janine a horrible lie. Elizabeth told her that we'd been having an affair."

"No..."

"She lured her out of our home with a phone call," Jake went on. "She told Janine she wanted to come clean about our affair." Jake paused, winced. "That was the night. The night Janine left, telling me she was heading to her parents'. That's why she had crossed the bridge into New Jersey when she told me she was heading to Albany. That's why I sensed she was upset when she...when she left..."

Jake's voice trailed off on a choked sob. Salina shifted her body forward and pulled him against her chest, held him as he let out his pent-up emotion.

"The last thing I wanted was for Elizabeth to lash out at

you because we were together. That's why I thought…I figured walking away…I didn't want anything to happen to you."

Salina held him tighter, feeling every ounce of his pain. "Nothing's gonna happen to me."

"If only I'd told Janine that Elizabeth wasn't over me… she would have known better when she called. She wouldn't have had to lose her life because of me."

Salina eased back, looked into Jake's tortured eyes. "Is that what you think? That this is your fault?"

"I should have told Janine about Elizabeth. If I'd told her—"

"What happened isn't your fault," Salina said, stressing the words. "Don't blame yourself for something that was out of your control. I'm certain Janine wouldn't want you to beat yourself up over this."

"If only she'd trusted our love, not let Elizabeth fill her head with lies."

Salina framed Jake's face with both hands. "She was human. She was fooled by a cunning liar. Yes, she should have known that you would never betray her, but she had a moment of weakness. That's not your fault, Jake. It's not."

Leaning forward, Salina kissed Jake's cheek. Then she wrapped her arms around him and hugged him, hoping to ease his mental suffering.

"Thank you," Jake said after a while. "Thank you for saying that."

"I mean it. It's not your fault." She paused, tightened her arms around his strong body. "And I'll tell you one thing— don't you worry about Elizabeth where I'm concerned. Trust me, I'll be ready for her if she tries anything."

Jake pulled out of Salina's embrace and stared down at her.

"I mean that," Salina told him.

"I know you do." A smile touched his lips. "You're strong. A fighter. Incredible."

"And a bit of a klutz," Salina added, smiling sheepishly.

"Ever since I got the call from the hospital and realized I couldn't lose you, it came to me what I need to do where Elizabeth is concerned. I'm going to send her a strongly worded letter full of legalese—make sure she knows she'll face jail time if she comes near me, you or Riquet."

"Good."

"And there's something else," Jake went on. "My mother."

"Oh," Salina said, her chest tightening.

"She's also not going to be a problem again. When I called her to see if she could watch Riquet, I had it out with her. I told her that from this point forward, she was never to get involved in my personal affairs. That I love her, but she was beyond rude to you. And I told her that as worried as she is about my public image, she needn't be. I've decided that I won't be entering the political arena."

"Jake?" Salina asked, hoping he hadn't come to that decision because of her.

"It wasn't my dream," he said. "It was my mother's. Seeing you in the hospital, knowing I could have lost you…well, it reinforced for me what's important. And that's a family life. Riquet has barely had access to me, I've been working so much. That has to change. It did change—because of you. You've been a huge blessing in my life…the ray of sunshine breaking through the clouds of gray."

"Oh, Jake. I'm going to cry."

"And don't think that when you marry me I'll expect you to stay home and be a caregiver. I want to help you see your dream of becoming a chef come true."

"What?"

"Culinary school—"

"No. What you said before that. About me marrying you?"

"I did say something about that, didn't I?" Jake asked with a coy smile. "I suppose I should have asked you. Will you marry me? We don't have to rush into it, we can have a long engagement, but—"

"Yes!" Salina exclaimed, giddy with happiness. And then she threw herself forward and planted her mouth on his.

The kiss grew hot within seconds, their tongues tangling in a dance as old as time.

Jake broke the kiss and looked down at her. "Your foot. You're supposed to—"

"This is what I'm supposed to do," she replied, and laid another hot kiss on him.

She gripped his wide shoulders, purred into his mouth as her need for him grew to a fever pitch. She wasn't an invalid. And she certainly was able to use the parts of her body that were thrumming with desire. She wanted to make love to Jake. And she wanted to do it right now.

Salina's lips parted on a sigh, and sweet heat pooled between her legs when Jake's tongue delved deep into her mouth.

Everything about him was intoxicating. One touch from him, one kiss, and she was totally turned on.

"Salina…"

"Make love to me," she said in a commanding voice, cutting Jake off. "The part of me that needs you, desires you, is perfectly fine. At least it will be, once you're in my bed."

Salina almost didn't recognize herself. Where Jake was concerned, she had become a wild woman. The kind who went after what she wanted. She didn't know what it was about him that brought out this side of her, but something did. Her need for him was so great that she couldn't deny herself.

But it was more than simply a physical need. It was love. He pressed his hands against her back and Salina moaned into his mouth. Then she slipped her hands beneath the hem of her T-shirt and pulled it over her head. No sooner than she had it off, she also removed her bra, letting her breasts spill free.

Jake groaned as his eyes swept over her. It was a reaction that Salina would never tire of. His groan grew deeper as he cupped her breasts and kissed her more ferociously.

Suddenly Jake's hands were on the waist of her jeans, unbuttoning them. Gingerly, he took them off her body, being extra careful when he pulled the leg over her injured foot. Next he removed her panties, doing so more hurriedly now. And once she was naked before him, he wasted no time spreading her thighs and bringing his mouth down on her most sensitive spot.

The sensations were as glorious as the first time. His tongue drove her crazy, each heated stroke so delicious Salina could only arch her back and moan in ecstasy. Soon she was shuddering, wave after wave of pleasure assaulting her body.

Jake kissed a path over her skin to her mouth, where he framed her face and kissed her deeply, tenderly. Kissed her as if to prove to her just how much she meant to him.

"Oh, Jake. I love you. I love you so much."

"I love you, too, sweetheart."

And when he positioned himself between her thighs, joining their bodies and making them one, Salina knew without a doubt that she had found the man of her dreams.

Because every stroke, every kiss, was full of meaning. Every stroke, every kiss, was full of love.

The kind of love that would last forever.

Salina knew that in her heart.

* * * * *

REQUEST YOUR FREE BOOKS!

2 FREE NOVELS
PLUS 2 FREE GIFTS!

KIMANI™
ROMANCE

Love's ultimate destination!

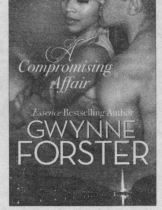